Eye of the Agency

ALSO BY RICHARD MOQUIST

The Franklin Mysteries

RICHARD MOQUIST

Eye of the Agency

◆ *A Sadie Greenstreet Mystery* ◆

St. Martin's Press
New York

Design by Ellen R. Sasahara

Library of Congress Cataloging-in-Publication Data

Moquist, Richard.
    Eye of the agency : a Sadie Greenstreet mystery / Richard Moquist. —1st ed.
        p.   cm.
    ISBN 0-312-15526-3
    I. Title.
PS3563.O695E96   1997
813'.54—dc21   97-6272
                                                                   CIP

First Edition: July 1997

10 9 8 7 6 5 4 3 2 1

FOR BARBARA

The author would like to thank the following for their assistance: The Pinkerton Agency for use of their logo and the Western History Collections, University of Oklahoma Library for use of the picture of Marshall Thurmond. All other prints and photographs are courtesy of the Library of Congress collection.

Special thanks to Dan Sadowski for historical research.

Thanks also to Trevor Hurley, Phil Carlson, and Ann Sadowski for editing and commentary, to Amanda Moquist for word processing, and Ben Moquist for computer graphics.

CONTENTS

Eye of the Agency

ENTER THE
PINKERTON MAN

———◆·◆·◆———

I t should have been, to paraphrase Dickens, the best of times, and, though it was far from the worst, I could not help but feel something was missing. Life had taken a turn some years back—a sudden turn, like a leaf just off the rapids finding itself among a hundred other leaves in slow-moving backwater. I was just now beginning to see that life is best on the rapids.

Those early years with my husband Horace were always an adventure. Days were filled with travel and the nights, I must confess, were filled with a bit of larceny. But, just as grey overtook our temples, respectability overtook us by degrees, and Horace accepted work with, of all organizations, the Pinkerton Investigation Agency. My husband's exploits with that illustrious firm have long been chronicled in newspapers from Chicago to St. Louis and, I have heard, all the way to New York—perhaps beyond. But always in those accounts he has been referred to discreetly as "an undisclosed Pinkerton agent."

From his first case some eleven years past—protecting President Lincoln from enemies during a zigzag sixteen-hundred-mile train ride from Illinois to the Capitol—to his famous uncovering of the great grain scandal in Chicago, the particulars of his many cases and the methods used to solve them remain to this day tucked neatly in the Pinkerton Agency file books.

Not that he hasn't been handsomely rewarded for his anonymous work. On the contrary, the Agency and others have kept us in comfort, if not extravagance. But my own part in that adventuresome life has been limited to the now-and-then cases taken on in our hometown of Chicago. Indeed, I found myself growing a bit impatient with his more than frequent absences, and just a trifle resentful of my increasingly limited role.

Being a distant relative of the patriot Thomas Paine, I have inherited his penchant for writing and, hopefully, some degree of his common sense as well. I have, for some years, kept myself occupied exercising these two modest qualities in my weekly advice column for the *Chicago Tribune*.

But it was my younger sister, Pamela, who first suggested I travel with Horace and keep a record of his cases. "Suggested" may not be the precise word. Horace had just returned from a three-month investigation of the infamous Ashby shootings in Cleveland. He had returned on the midnight train and hadn't yet risen the morning Pamela came knocking at my door with a determined look on her face.

"Sadie Greenstreet," she said without preamble, tossing her corded silk bonnet onto a chair with the same exhilaration a slave might throw off his fetters. "Where have I been, you ask?"

I hadn't, but knew I would soon find out. Standing there, tall and statuesque in a dress of royal blue, she looked very much like a painting after the style of Gainsborough. Her ebony hair was accentuated by three circle tresses of the French fashion, one on either temple and the third just left-center of her forehead. Her face was slightly pale, except when excited. She was excited now.

"A meeting of the Illinois chapter of the Women's Suffrage Society," she declared, bowing slightly as if expecting applause. "That is where I've been."

I set my volume of Whitman on the side table and, after pouring two cups of sassafras tea, I rested my cheeks on open palms, preparing for the inevitable details of Pamela's latest enlightenment. She had, in the past, organized bazaars for relief after the great Chicago fire; stood side-by-side with the Knights of Labor and their newly unionized garment workers when they struck in '72; and stormed the gates of the Kennecutt packinghouse, rescuing sixteen child laborers. If this was like her other causes, she would enter into the struggle with energy rampant.

She did not disappoint. Pamela paced to and fro like a thoroughbred awaiting the gun. At length, using Horace's stuffed easy chair as a lectern, she began.

"It's high time we acted, Sadie. Do you realize it's been ten years since President Lincoln emancipated the slaves? And now here we are, little better off than they were then. We have no vote, cannot own property, cannot obtain a divorce; it is intolerable. Look at your own situation, Sadie."

"What on earth do you mean, my situation?"

"Oh, come, come now. All this reading and your 'Ask

Sadie' column are only diversions." She paused as her eyes caught a glimpse of Horace's derby hanging on a wall peg. "I know you are only happy when you're poking about in Horace's inquiries. I see he is home, but you can be certain that in no time he'll be off again. And you will . . ."

Pamela lifted my book from the side table, fanned its pages, then closed it hard, as if to make a point. "While Horace is out seeing the world, you are sentenced merely to sit at home and read of that world. But that's the way it's always been, Sadie," she said, shaking her head. "And why?"

I had no answer, so she continued, finger pointing to the ceiling. "Because we lack the backbone to stand up and voice our demands!"

Pamela proceeded, speaking now of Julia Howe, of liberalism, socialism, reform. But I heard only snatches of her words. Out of the corner of my eye, I saw Horace standing by the upstairs balustrade, hands on hips.

Still a handsome man at forty, he was just now beginning to show his age. His forehead had moved an inch north from where it once had been. Thick, gold-rimmed spectacles now partially hid his dark brown eyes. Greying side whiskers and a confident air had transformed his look from boyish to bankish.

Presently Pamela's eyes followed mine, and pallor came to her face when she saw we were not alone. The sound of Horace's clapping hands resounded round the high-ceilinged parlor as he descended the staircase.

"Bravo, Pamela! A fine cause. I'm all for the rights of women. The fact of the matter is, I've convinced Mr.

Pinkerton to hire several women operatives of late," he said, with a circumspect glance, "and we always contribute to the unwed mothers' fund."

Pamela, quick as always with a comeback, was at no loss for words. "Well then, Mr. Horace Thaddeus Greenstreet, why do you allow your wife to live the life she does? Why is she not among these new operatives?"

Horace's forehead colored slightly as he nervously brushed each side of his moustache with a thumbnail. The only other person who ever used Horace's middle name was his mother, and the intent was not lost on him. He stood up straight for an instant as if being scolded for posture. He turned toward me again, this time plaintively. Pamela continued. "She sits at home and reads while you are off to Kansas City or St. Paul or who knows where else. Last Tuesday I came for a visit, and she was curled up with the *Encyclopedia Britannica*. The *Encyclopedia Britannica,* for God's sake!"

I nearly protested at that moment, but checked myself and held my tongue, eager to hear Horace's reply. It was true, I felt stifled and static at times. Yet, there was something comfortable about my life, like an old easy chair you know should be abandoned yet still hang onto. I felt Pamela speaking for the part of me who wanted to discard that old chair.

"We have always been equals in this house," he said at last.

"We were once on equal terms, but today . . ." I shrugged to give a more pronounced effect to my words. "Today, I am not so certain."

Horace puffed himself up to full height, a height that nearly matched that of Pamela. A quiet sort of tension grew for several seconds. The old brass mantel clock ticked loudly and rhythmically in the silence. As Horace pursed his lips and began to lift his hand as a prelude to speech, I jerked with a start. The knocker on the front door sounded, loudly and continuously.

Whether it is Fate or Providence that brings together two unrelated incidents and so changes one's life, I cannot say. Horace would say Fate, for he is a freethinker; I am a nominal Presbyterian and am inclined toward the latter. Nonetheless, the decision of Pamela to attend a suffrage meeting and her subsequent visit to our house was followed by a second, unrelated visit, and the two together marked great changes in my life. Without a word, Horace walked brusquely to the door and spoke briefly to a messenger boy, before filling the young man's open palm with several small coins. Horace gave us a secretive over-the-shoulder squint upon closing the door, and we watched as he read the dispatch.

When he had finished, I saw clearly the truth of Pamela's words. I had lost him again. The man who had arrived late last night with chocolates in one hand and a bottle of claret in the other had vanished. The man whom I had stayed up with into the small hours, discussing everything but his mission to Cleveland, was nowhere to be found.

The transformation had began slowly. Horace set two sheets of paper, one large and one small, on his writing desk. He rolled a cigarette the way he always did—just as the old Dutchman of his company had taught him during the war. The fingers on his left hand meditatively drummed the desk while his right deftly put together paper and Turkish tobacco in a shape that can best be described as resembling an English hunting horn. On the cigarette's completion, he lit the wide end and drew in deeply. The change was complete. He was now no longer my husband, but a Pinkerton man. And, soon again, I would be a Pinkerton widow.

II

THE EYE OF
THE AGENCY

———•◆•———

The two papers came from a large, cream-colored envelope that bore an unmistakable red seal in the shape of an eye. Quite probably they were from Mr. Allan Pinkerton himself.

The fingers on Horace's left hand walked nervously up and down his cheek. Pamela sent a glance my way that asked if she should leave. I replied with a shake of the head and strode to Horace's side.

"Trouble?" I asked. Horace nodded solemnly but did not speak.

"I don't suppose it's local trouble," I said, not attempting to conceal the irritation in my voice.

Horace lifted his eyes in a pained expression. "I know I promised, and I wouldn't think of leaving again." He paused, gazing ruefully at the smaller of the two sheets of paper, then thrust it into my hand. "By God, Sadie! What am I to do?"

The note was neatly typewritten on penny paper. In the center of the page were the words:

I WILL SHOW THAT NOTHING CAN HAPPEN MORE
BEAUTIFUL THAN DEATH.

"Is it meant . . . for you?" I tried not to show alarm in
my voice.

"No, no Sadie. The letter is for . . ." Horace looked up,
realizing we were not alone. He rose slowly from his desk,
avoiding any contact with my eyes, and dropped weight-
ily into the parlor chair with a sigh. "This concerns a client
I shall call Mr. Jones so as not to breach a confidence. I shall
tell you his story and leave it to you whether I should take
his case." Horace continued as I took a seat next to Pamela.
"It appears Mr. Jones owns a riverboat steamer company.
He received an offer to buy his principal showboat about
a month ago from a Mr. Brown, who owns a rival riverboat concern. Now, Mr. Brown has, in the past, bought up
several small passenger steamers using a business tech-
nique which can best be described as strong-arming. It is
believed that he is attempting to monopolize the business.
Shortly after Mr. Jones declined the offer, a first threatening letter was received. It was unfortunately thought to be
a prank and destroyed. This second letter," Horace pointed
to the one I was now holding, "was received a week later,
and, since that time, Mr. Brown's business practices have
become better known to Mr. Jones, leading him to believe
the threat could well be genuine. He wishes a Pinkerton
man to investigate the origins of the note and to protect
him if necessary. Mr. Jones's showboat leaves Cincinnati tomorrow for a trip to St. Louis. Mr. Brown has requested
another meeting and plans to rendezvous with the show-

boat in Cairo, Illinois, where the Ohio meets the Mississippi."

While Horace spoke, I had been studying the square
of paper and its threatening message. "Typed on a Sholes
typewriter," I mused. I was beginning to get an idea. It was
just possible that a bit of common sense was the very thing
this case required.

Horace looked at Pamela and then me. "The matter
may be of the greatest importance, but I am a man of my
word, and a promise is a promise. Again I say, I shall leave
it to you whether I should take the case."

Pamela sat in her chair, pretending to peruse my book,
while humming softly "The Battle Hymn of the Repub-
lic," a song I later learned had become a rallying song of
the suffragists' union.

"Perhaps *we* should take the case," I offered.

"You cannot seriously wish to accompany me, Sadie."

"Not if you think it would hinder your investigation,
Horace. But perhaps I can convince you my presence
would be useful." Pamela ceased humming. Horace removed his reading glasses and listened.

"You see, Horace, a man's mind is, for the most part, a
factual, logical one, and, in your profession, this is most important. But a woman's mind excels at something else:
reading people, why they act as they do. We trust our feelings, our intuitive hunches. Now, when you read this letter, you saw it as a threat to a client and concentrated on
the facts presented to you. I, however, can tell you a great
deal about the person who wrote it."

Horace moved uncomfortably in his red brocade chair.

I proceeded. "First, the note is typed on an early Sholes typewriter. This is revealed by the characteristic boxy

capitals. Second, the characters are uniform; that is to say, none of the letters appear more bold than any others, signifying someone skilled at the art of typing. Since the typewriter has only been in wide use for the last five or six years, people who have achieved that level of skill are few and far between.

"Next," I said, drawing some confidence from Horace's intent expression, "consider the fact that the note is perfectly centered on the page. And it certainly is an unusual way to phrase a threat. It is almost poetic. I would venture that the person is not only well-educated but also fastidious. Finally, the writer is probably neither poor nor well off, for the paper used is of a modest quality penny stock." I lifted the paper near a table lantern to show there was no watermark. "This conclusion, however, is a trifle less certain than the others, since a rich man with tight purse strings might also be inclined to purchase a modest-priced paper.

"So, if I were investigating, I would be seeking someone who is meticulous in habits and well-trained in mind. A middle-class individual who is also a skilled typist."

"Bravo!" cried Pamela, hands clapping in a parody of Horace's previous gesture.

When Horace's jaw returned to its normal position, he snuffed out a newly lighted cigarette and stood in front of the chair I now occupied. He held that position for thirty-odd seconds before speaking. "I know when I am beaten. You may be sorry, Sadie, and I am quite certain I will be, but if you insist on coming with me, I shall not deny you. And," he offered with a philosophic shrug, "I must confess that a river ride on a showboat, while keeping watch over its owner, does appear as unhazardous a duty as one could hope for. It may be that the assignment will involve no more than keeping a protective eye on an overly nervous businessman; it may be far less dangerous than attending a rally of Pamela's suffragists."

Horace's voice became firm as he continued. "This will not be like the old days, Sadie. I am a Pinkerton man now, and I will need to take full responsibility for your actions as well as my own. Furthermore, this is not a holiday lark but business—business of a potentially serious nature." He hesitated for a moment. "But, if you will heed and abide by these points, I see no reason why you should not accompany me.

"It is now nearly noon," he announced, clicking his silver pocket watch shut. "I must consult with the superintendent and arrange train passage to Cincinnati. I'm sure you have arrangements of your own to make."

Pamela and I stood before him like two grenadier cadets receiving their first orders, but, when the door finally closed behind him, she grabbed my arm with a high-pitched laugh.

Had a Tom-peep looked through the parlor window that very moment, I do believe he'd have walked away with head shaking and called us mad. Pamela's feet did a little jig, and we both danced about the room like schoolgirls.

"A person meticulous in habits who is well-educated and very probably middle-class," Pamela mimicked. "For a moment I thought you were describing Horace himself." She laughed again as we grabbed each other's hands.

"I suggest," interrupted a firm but familiar voice coming from the direction of the front door, "we end the frivolity and put our minds to getting ready for our trip." Horace retrieved his brown felt derby from its peg. The door closed again, just in time to receive the full force of two divan pillows thrown squarely at its center.

III

OF FIREWORKS AND
CHAMPAGNE

I t seems to me that there are three types of people in this world—those on stage, those in the audience, and those who do not bother to attend the performance. The first are the adventurous sort, like sister Pamela, always pushing fate or even making their own. There are only a scarce few in this camp and always they are the most interesting. Horace also is among their number, his silver Pinkerton's badge a constant symbol and reminder. Once, I too was one.

Then, there are those who take a laissez-faire attitude, neither shrinking from nor testing their destiny, but rather accepting, like a grim Calvinist, whatever life brings. In this camp lie the great throngs of humanity.

Finally, there are those who withdraw from life, insulating themselves from the world by means of locked doors or laudanum drops. I had taken the first steps in escaping this later group when Horace agreed that I should accompany him on this trip. Pamela had made it sound as if I were standing up for women, not myself—as if it were my duty to travel with Horace and share his adventures.

But, as the train moved further and further from home, I grew more and more uncertain and apprehensive.

The Chesapeake and Ohio Line makes the Chicago to Cincinnati run twice a day; as we sat in a smoker car on the evening train, Horace began to explain the particulars of his assignment. July twilight had given way to darkness, and we could no longer be entertained by the rolling hills and forests or charmed by the farmland of the Illinois countryside. When even the monotonous telegraph poles faded from view, Horace drew out his smoking paraphernalia and began his ritual rolling of the cigarette. I have, for some odd reason, always found fascination in their adept manufacture and often speculate, while they are being created, on what the end-product will look like. Tonight's sculpture was straighter than most, though fat at one end and roughly resembling a crooked sugar spoon.

"Our client, Mr. Jones, is really Mr. Elcid Hardacre, a self-made enterpriser who earned his pile in the riverboat trade. Hardacre has received two threatening letters, one of which we have seen; for reasons not perfectly clear, he is convinced they were written by Andrew DuBois, a St. Louis man also in the steamboat business. DuBois, it seems, has made an offer for Mr. Hardacre's flagship, the *Mississippi Girl*. There is a meeting of Hardacre and DuBois planned for the town of Cairo on the fourth. So, tomorrow," Horace said, handing me an itinerary and map of the Ohio and Mississippi, "we shall be flying down the Ohio on, what I am told, is the finest of river showboats."

I closed my eyes, recalling the dream I had last night. I was traveling down a long corridor and, when I got to its end, there was no door, only a high window just out of reach. I jumped, as one can only do in a dream, floating high in the air before returning softly to the ground. When I looked through the high window I saw a familiar room, but one it seemed I hadn't visited in years.

The room was filled with delightful things—ponies, carnival clowns, and booths selling candy apples and licorice. Then the scene changed slightly, the window became a door, and I held in my hand a great gold key. I tried the key in the lock and found it fit perfectly. But an unexplained panic overtook me, and instead of opening the door I placed the key in my pocket, returning the way I came, down the long lonely corridor.

The setting sun had not brought relief from the sultry, stagnant air of the smoking car, and I fanned myself liberally with the map. With all sleeping cars occupied, I sighed with resignation on contemplating the ride ahead in that dreary compartment.

Tobacco and time had done its work on the once elegant smoker car, I thought to myself. A red clay jardiniere stood near the forward door, displaying a rather yellowed

Louisiana fern, which, by all indications, had been used all too freely as a spittoon. Meanwhile, a four-foot cuspidor guarded the rear door, showing little sign of use. The cloth seats were threadbare, the windows dull and sooty, and even the mural, which ran the length of the car over the windows, depicting some mythical hunting scene, had lost its color. Watching Horace glare about, I was sure he was as eager to find more hospitable quarters as I was.

A man with white shirt sleeves rolled up to the elbows made his way from the forward dining car. He had iced lemonade in hand, the sight of which must have set Horace's mind to working. "The Fourth of July," Horace murmured to himself. His eyes gleamed the scampish gleam of a boy regarding an unwatched pie. In an instant, he was gone to a rear compartment, then returned and passed quickly on to a forward coach. It was some five minutes before he returned again, this time with a dark-skinned porter at his heels. Words were exchanged, and the porter left with a toothy smile, admiring the dollar bill Horace had slipped into his hand. Horace stood before me, tipping his hat. "Horace T. Greenstreet, purveyor of pyrotechnics," he said, measuring each word slowly as if trying them on for size. He repeated those words, this time with a slight Dixie drawl. His hand held a quicksilver thermometer, which he read at arm's length over the top of gold-rimmed eyeglasses. "Ninety-two degrees," he said, shaking his head. "Very bad. Very bad, indeed."

Presently, and before I could question his strange behavior, the porter reentered the car and announced our table was ready.

"Table?"

Horace merely smiled and held out his hand.

The bill of fare in the dining car was longer than I expected, but Horace did not seem at all interested in deviled eggs or smoked ham. He studied minutely the faces of the couple seated across from us. The man who doted on his wife's every word was wiry and businesslike in dress and manner. But it wasn't he who attracted my attention.

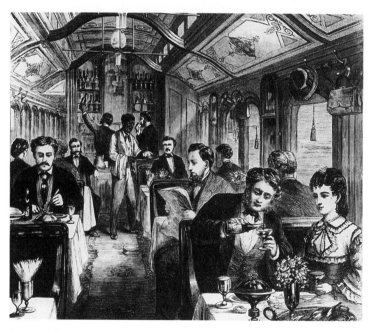

It was his wife. She was narrow-eyed and pinch-faced, with a frame inclined towards corpulence. She wore rouge, too much rouge, in a color and intensity unsuited for daylight. A gaudy, out-of-style hat was perched on her puffed

hair. The hat was the peach-basket variety with two ludi-
crous ostrich feathers at either side that curled around
from back to front. She sat stiff as the horsehair crinoline
it was made of, taking her food in thrifty bites without
seeming to enjoy it.

I must admit, at this point, that I have three vices. My
affinity for hats is the one I most freely acknowledge without reservation or apologies. Hats of any shape or style,
color, or material, plain or stylish; they all hold a fascination. My first and most lasting impression of a woman is
nearly always gained by a study of her headgear.

There was more than just the woman's hat to dislike I
thought, as she berated her husband for the way he han-
dled his silver. I watched by way of a sidewise glance as she
dropped a glass salt shaker into her waiting reticule. I
thought to myself that, if the year had been 1853 rather
than 1873, she might have found herself victim of a particular sharper and his cunning young shill. And to my de-
light, I found twenty years had not changed Horace
altogether.

He spoke to me in a whisper, a whisper just loud
enough for all around us to hear. "Your final destination
is Cincinnati, I understand."

"Well," I hesitated, "as a matter of fact . . ."

"Splendid!" Horace interrupted. "Then you shall be
able to witness the finest fireworks display this side of the
China Sea. The riverfront of Cincinnati will be lit up with
the thunder and flashes of a night sky over Vicksburg."

"You don't say."

"I do, I do. I've got half a boxcar back there filled to the ceiling with the stuff—flying candles, screamers, and flash-bombs; you name it, and it's back there." Horace pulled out the thermometer, scrutinizing it with a concerned look while Mrs. Gaudy Hat bent her ear.

"Isn't it a dangerous business—transporting fireworks, I mean?"

"Tricky is the word. Yes, tricky, not always dangerous. Just keep the temperature down when moving your cargo; that's the way. Haven't had an incident in our last seven orders."

"Just where is this boxcar full of fireworks?" I asked, as we made a concordat with our eyes, and I grew into my role.

"Just back of the last sleeper car. But don't you be worrying none."

The wheels rattled against the rails, but that was the only sound. Indeed, the passengers had grown so quiet one would have imagined the lot of them had been taken with lockjaw. Horace looked to his watch. A few began to speak in low voices, but most strained their ears like so many greedy gossipmongers waiting by the back fence for the newest rumor.

The rear coach door sprang open suddenly and all watched the porter scramble to Horace's side and whisper in his ear.

"Great Scott! This is terrible! Bring water and ice!" Horace told the porter, then bolted out the rear door.

I adjusted my crushed velvet hat. I smiled genteelly at

the now-and-again questioning glances of my fellow travelers. I tried my best to convey just a touch of distress as I averted my eyes.

The clicking of the points and the staccato chugging of the engine indicated that we were nearing a station. "Indianapolis," the conductor cried, as the brakes were set and we began slowing to a stop. Hurried pow-wows were held at every table, the results of which left four of the ten dining car passengers heading for the platform and the remainder taking refuge in the more forward drawing coach.

A crooked, red-nailed finger waggled near the face of the conductor, its owner's nostrils flaring like a war horse in winter. "The management will hear of this; you can be assured. This is a passenger train. The very idea of transporting dangerous explosives," said the woman with the milliner's misdemeanor on her head. "Come along, Clarence. We will take our business elsewhere."

Astonished, the conductor shot a quizzical glance in my direction. I only shrugged.

By and by the conductor discovered there were unexpected vacancies in the sleeping car. The open-handed conductor assured us that this was only due to his own prodigious efforts. He stood palm facing upward waiting for our tribute; Horace sighed, but in the end placed four bits in the waiting hand.

As we sipped champagne in the coolness of the well-vented sleeper, Horace lifted his glass. "Here is to the old days," he said.

Iron wheels whirled and churned, pounding across rail and tie, propelling us ever closer to a shared adventure. Tomorrow it would be the paddle wheel's turn. Our glasses touched. "And, here is to the new," said I.

Horace threw his hat onto the bunk then, looking at his reflection in the window, tried his latest alias on for size one more time. "Horace T. Greenstreet, purveyor of pyrotechnics."

I trimmed the lantern and took the glass from his hand, placing it on the sleeper car floor. "I'll be the judge of that," I said.

IV

THE MISSISSIPPI GIRL

The *Mississippi Girl* was long and trim, a handsome boat painted in white with crisp red ornamentations and lettering. Its bow was adorned with a carved figure of a young girl in the manner of ancient sea galleons, its railings festooned with crimson bunting. Two fancy-rimmed black chimneys puffed out a stately nimbus of equally black smoke as the boat's departure bells faded in the rush and roar of the great steam engine. The landing stage was lifted. Paddle wheels geared and groaned into action as wharf hands with poles began pushing the stern-wheeler away from the dock moorings. Horace removed his derby, waving it like the other passengers crowding the rails of the promenade deck. I joined in the charade, assuming my part as a woman of leisure, and waved my handkerchief. But one-by-one the passengers quit those send-off waves and began pointing at a curious sight. A narrow fellow of perhaps twenty-five with a dark Ulysses beard was dodging his way around barrels and around people. He was heading down the wharf walk at break-neck speed, waving his left hand while in his right swung a large traveling satchel.

"He'll never make it," the man next to me snorted. Horace gave the speaker an uncertain look.

Above the clamor, we heard the man faintly cry the word "Stop." But there was no stopping the *Mississippi Girl*. The bearded man halted at the edge of the dock for a second only. Dropping his traveling bag, he stepped back four steps. The leap that followed traversed some six feet of water and was nearly unsuccessful, for the man's feet now hung precariously on the edge of the steerage deck. The man's arms were swinging wildly in circles like gust-driven windmills, and his black top hat dropped into the river. Just then, amid gasps and holdings of breath, a uniformed man who had been collecting tickets on the starboard entrance grabbed the now-hatless man's arm and pulled him aboard.

The bearded man's traveling bag was heaved on deck by a bare-chested stevedore, and when the quick-thinking newcomer reached for a grapnel hook and retrieved his top hat from the brackish levee water, the crowd let out a roar of relief and approval.

The frantic scene was over. The passengers, now in even higher spirits, returned to their waves. The new arrival shook hands all around, then joined in the revelry. A crewman hoisted up the jackstaff, a thirty-seven starred flag that unfurled and flapped in the breeze. With pitch-smoke billowing, paddle wheel churning, the *Mississippi Girl* was on her way.

"He's a bit of a wag, but sharp as a pin."

"I beg your pardon?" I said to the square-jawed man standing at our side. He was the perfect picture of a middle-aged riverboat dandy, with a white ruffled shirt starched at the collar, a mulberry swallow-tail jacket, and a black string tie. His smile was broad and showed nearly as much gold as the ring on my left hand. His speech was dandified as well, a curious mixture of Western dialect and high English that would have made a Missouri senator proud. After regarding us briefly, he turned back to the well-wishers and tipped his Western hat.

"You are from Chicago, are you not?" he said, not looking at us.

"We are," Horace affirmed.

"The two men sent by Mr. P?"

I gave a slight blush and looked to Horace, after making sure I was still wearing my green brocade dress.

Horace smiled. "The same. And who is sharp as a pin?"

"I was referring to the damned fool on the steerage deck with the wet top hat." The stranger pointed below to the man who had caused all the commotion. "I should have known he would make it aboard. His name is Allan Culbertson, my clerk and ship's purser. The man is a cat. You throw him out of a two-story window, and nine times out of ten he'll land on his feet. But never mind him." He turned on his heels with the air of a Union soldier. "Attendant!" he shouted to an eager-faced boy of fourteen or fifteen standing nearby. "Take these people's traveling bags to stateroom C." I watched with some disquietude as the boy struggled with my overstuffed trunk, the one Horace called Noah's Ark, my paperboard hat boxes, and Horace's small satchel. "We can talk more privately in my own state-room," the stranger said.

We followed in the wake of his long, colorful coattails, climbing spiral stairs to the uppermost regions of the boat, which, in river parlance, is known as the texas deck. Located just beneath the windowed pilot house was a fair-sized social room and the large first-class berths. Passing down a long corridor, we soon found our way to the largest of eight staterooms. A dark, almost gloomy room, it was furnished mainly with black mahogany and hair cloth chairs and tables whose arms and legs were carved into the shape of lion's paws. The room was drab as monk's cloth, the kind only a man could find attractive. The pervading atmosphere was close. The acrid smell of stale tobacco smoke, mixed with a hint of bay rum, fairly stung my nose and eyes.

On a wall were two crossed Springfield muskets, just the kind that Horace himself owned. "As you may have gathered, I am Mr. Elcid Hardacre," said the man slightly out of breath. Horace stepped forward, extending a right hand, and the two men shook hands just beneath the rifle stocks. "I am Horace Greenstreet, and this is Sadie Green-street, my wife and associate." The riverboat owner looked my way a good deal longer than seemed appropriate, a lingering look that seemed to say, "Married, eh? That is unfortunate."

Mr. Hardacre stood by a side board and began pouring a blood-red liquid into three tall glasses. It was a good four fingers, and it was not yet noon. Perhaps he was testing my reaction; perhaps it was just his way. I could not yet tell, so I took the liquor graciously. Lifting it close to my face, I gave Horace a cross-eyed look over the rim. Hardacre drained his glass of the fortified wine in one motion. *"In vino veritas,"* he said, holding up the empty glass.

Noticing the blank look engendered on Horace's face by the unfamiliar phrase, I intervened. "I am not accustomed to this much truth before noon," I said, taking a small sip from my glass.

Hardacre nodded with a pleased expression on his face, then turned to Horace. "I understand you prefer to work, as they say, under false colors."

"It is the policy of the Agency to remain anonymous whenever possible."

"Good. Then, for the purpose of our business, you shall be a Chicago solicitor whom I have engaged. Does that suit you?"

"If you wish," Horace replied.

After filling his own glass a second time, he motioned us to two small cushion chairs.

"I am not a man easily frightened," he said, taking a chair close to me. "But neither am I a fool. What we have here is intimidation, pure and simple." Our client looked thoughtfully into his glass. "I take it you have already been given a sketch of the objectives of your employment?"

"We have."

"Then what else do you wish to know, Mr. Greenstreet?"

"Have you taken the threatening letter and your story to the authorities?"

Mr. Hardacre answered with a resounding baritone laugh. "Authorities, you say. And just which authorities should I notify?" He pointed out the porthole. "There is Kentucky. On the opposite shore is Ohio, and tomorrow we will be in Illinois. The firm of DuBois and Sutton, whom I suspect to be behind this business, is located in St. Louis. Our final destination is also St. Louis. Who, then, should I notify? Who has jurisdiction over the Ohio and Mississippi? This is my home, Mr. Greenstreet." He waved his right hand to indicate the stateroom before bringing the left down soundly on a side table. "Furthermore, I have no stomach for any blue-hat rascals snooping about in my affairs."

Horace had nearly completed work on a cigarette, and I played my little game, judging it most like a Napoleon hat. "You can be assured," he said after striking a wooden match, "that we will use the utmost discretion. But we will have to know a bit more about your business dealings."

Mr. Hardacre's eyes scanned the ceiling, as if searching for the proper place to begin. He arose, stepping toward the furthermost wall, and stood before a gilt-framed picture of a man who bore a striking resemblance to himself. The man in the painting had an imperious air, his dark eyes looking down from beneath a naval bicorne embellished with gold-fretted cords. For some reason, I got a feeling the hat was store-bought, the medals on his chest of the unearned variety. Our host spoke as if to the portrait, and the wine must have had its effect, for his voice was now tinged with medicated sentiment.

"My father was Clement Hardacre," he said at last.

"His was a great name on the Mississippi some thirty years past. Before the railroad, you know, when the steamboat was king. A man who owned a steamer in those days was considered wealthy; to own two was to be a prince. My father owned three, and the smallest stretched one hundred twenty feet from bow to wheel. Cotton and immigrants were their cargo going north, and grain returning south. Then the war came, and that took care of all steamboat trade for a good long time. Being too old for the fight, he got the notion in his head that it was his duty to keep the Union soldiers supplied. 'A man has scarcely a few chances in life to do something fine, something worthwhile, something to be remembered by,' he would tell me when I asked why he would risk everything he had worked for. Well, he was remembered," Hardacre said ironically. "Remembered as the man who got three fine steamers blown up in the space of two weeks, all his dreams gone with the Confederate cannonballs." Hardacre straightened the picture. He bit his lower lip as he turned away from the portrait. "Do you know what else he got for his worthwhile deeds?" he asked us with arms now crossed. "He got a bill from the Secretary of War charging him for government cargo lost on his steamboats. Can you beat that?"

"Was there no insurance on the three boats?" Horace asked.

"Underwriters do not pay for damages incurred by acts of war," he said, shaking his head, "and it was six months after the war's end before the government admitted their mistake. By then he was a tired man, and defeated by a war he had helped win. He died a year later." The eyes of our client appeared dull and remote as a crystal gazer, but presently he returned to his previous abrupt demeanor.

"So, as you can imagine, I was born with river water in my veins and with a distrust of government functionaries in my heart." He paused, and, while he again searched the ceiling beams for words, I considered the features of Mr. Elcid Hardacre carefully.

He was an intriguing man, to say the least. According to my best reckoning, just this side of thirty-five, maybe even less. His ruddy grog-blossom nose, the missing digit of his left hand, and his more than adequate waistline all testified that he had lived those thirty-odd years both hard and to the full. He had the characteristic square jaw of a kind the physiognomist would say indicated strength of character. But, for all that, I couldn't help but feel he was not as strong as he appeared. Perhaps it was those dull, remote eyes.

Hardacre continued. "And so I had to make a go of it myself. A few years ago it was a seven-high straight that won me two thousand dollars, enough to buy an interest in an old steam packet. That put the Hardacre name back in the business for which Fate seems to have created us. I parlayed one packet into two and, in time, had the capital to build this." He raised his left hand, palm up, to indicate the showboat. "So, I'm at least back to the state my father attained—with three boats on the river."

The *Mississippi Girl* must have turned a sharp bend in the river, for the sun suddenly poured in through the porthole window. Passing first through tree branches along the shore, the light flickered nervously about the room as if unaccustomed to the surroundings. The light illuminated the face of Mr. Hardacre. He scowled at the intrusion, his face revealing something deeper than his previous blunt, yet not altogether displeasing, demeanor. Before our host pulled back the curtains, I heard the faint cries of the leadsman giving his soundings from the bow of the steamboat, soundings such as I'd heard tales of. "Mark quarter plus twain . . . mark half plus twain," his voice droned, indicating increasingly deeper water.

I had no intentions of speaking, but suddenly heard my voice say, "It is inevitable that a successful man of any business will crush a few toes along his path. Are there any enemies from your past whom you suspect?"

I eagerly waited Mr. Hardacre's answer, not daring to look in Horace's direction. The room had returned to its former cheerless state, but I saw clearly a twitching of our client's eye and an uneasy expression pass over his countenance.

"As I stated in my letter," he said flatly, "it is my belief that the firm of DuBois and Sutton is behind this. To be exact, I believe it is Mr. Andrew DuBois himself."

"Well, we must at least consider all the possibilities," I replied, almost defensively.

Horace removed the threatening square of paper from his breast pocket. "How and where was this delivered?"

"We were waylaid a week in Cincinnati for repairs," Hardacre answered. "It was delivered there by a courier and not by post. That is why I am certain the firm of

DuBois and Sutton is behind this. You see, I received a similar note some weeks back by courier while we were docked in St. Louis. That was only days after Mr. DuBois had offered to buy my steamboat, and I had refused. A second offer then came, and, again, I turned it down. Days later, I received that message. A hand-delivered message indicates someone local," he added with finality, "and DuBois and Sutton have offices in both St. Louis and Cincinnati."

"A hand-delivered message in both St. Louis and Cincinnati might also indicate someone from your own boat," Horace offered.

The riverman furrowed his brow. "I do not pay the highest of wages, but river work is hard to come by, and I am quite certain each member of the crew is thankful for his billet."

"Has anyone been fired recently?"

Hardacre hesitated. "Captain McQuaid is making his final command on the *Mississippi Girl,* but I wouldn't say he is being fired. It is more of a mutual parting of the ways."

Hardacre had moved from a position directly in front of us and was now standing by my chair. I could feel his eyes studying the nape of my neck. His right hand momentarily rested on the arm of my chair, clearly revealing his missing ring finger.

Under other circumstances, I might have felt uneasy, frightened, or possibly even flattered. I looked to Horace, but his eyes were elsewhere, and I followed them to a shelf of books on the near wall. They appeared old but were neatly arranged in order of size. I could just make out the largest as being an *Oxford Dictionary*. Everything about the man seemed distant and mysterious: His fancy clothes and unsettling humor, his missing finger, his strange accent, his lonely and gloomy room; even those rows of ancient books seemed to inspire mystery. But, like a character from a Gothic novel, he remained disturbingly beguiling.

With a swaggering gait, the man returned to his chair. Before I could gather my thoughts and speculate on the true nature of the man, Horace asked the very question that was beginning to shape itself in my mind.

"You have spent a great deal of time in England, have you not?"

Hardacre appeared amused and gave him an acknowledging elevation of the brow.

"A year in preparatory school and four at Eton," he said. "They don't take well to those from the wrong side of the ocean, but I only had to bust a few heads to help them see it more my way. So I guess my father killed his two birds with one shot, as the saying goes. He got me educated and taught me to stand up for myself at the same time."

Horace changed the subject. "About that first note, which you unfortunately discarded. Was it typed or handwritten?"

"Typewritten, as I recall. But as I said, I paid it little heed."

"How exactly was the first threat worded?"

Hardacre considered his now-empty glass for a moment as if deciding whether to refill it. "I can't rightly recall it to mind. I believe there were some words about imminent danger. It wasn't until I heard about old Jack Bruce that I gave the matter some reflection." Hardacre ran his fingers through his hair. "Now, old Jack ran the *Prairie Clipper* out of Natchez. One day Jack was killed in a boiler explosion—not a big explosion, but it came just as they were stoking her up, and she was not under full pressure. That is more than unusual, you see: Boiler explosions usually wait for full steam so they can make a good job of it. Well, two weeks later, the *Clipper* is patched up and running again . . . registered to the firm of DuBois and Sutton.

"So, let's not be making more of this than need be," he continued. "The case is simple enough in my mind. I have agreed to a meeting with Colonel DuBois tomorrow in Cairo. And you will be there to protect me when I again refuse his offer."

"Colonel?"

"Yes. A Rebel colonel," he said scornfully.

A momentary vacuum of silence held the room. There were voices in the hallway, and again the faint cries of the leadsman could be heard. "Where did you spend your war years?" Horace asked.

Elcid Hardacre squared his shoulders but looked a bit embarrassed. "I was in England," he said finally. "And you?"

Horace smiled wryly. "Guarding the Western flank," he said. "Fort Santa Cruz, you know." It was Mr. Hardacre's turn for a vacant expression. "I was in California for much of the war," Horace explained, "and we did put together a company—even drew up plans for a march on Texas. But the plans were never approved."

At that moment, a shrill whistle sounded from somewhere in the cabin. Mr. Hardacre walked to his desk and spoke very loudly through one of three communication tubes. "Yes . . . yes . . . very well . . . yes . . . very well . . . Have Culbertson sent to my room in five minutes."

While Hardacre was conversing with his hollow tube, I rose to examine his bookcase. Running a finger down a line of leather-bound books, I found his tastes ranged from Milton to Adam Smith, from Homer to Bret Harte. They say a man's measure can be divined from the books he reads and the condition of those books. Unlike my own, these contained no bookmarks or even any signs of use. I was considering this fact when my attention was returned to the room. I watched in astonishment as Horace did a very peculiar thing. With the stealthy hand of a pickpocket, his fingers had moved to a nearby desk. As our client spoke his last word into the tube, Horace snatched a piece of writing paper from the bureau. In an instant, the paper was tucked in his breast pocket.

"Is there anything further you wish to know?" Hardacre said, again turning his attention to us.

Horace stood. "Notwithstanding your beliefs concerning the origins of this letter, I must insist we work, as they say, by the book. I would like a listing of all passengers and crew."

"As you wish. The case is simple enough by my way of thinking, but if you insist on making more of it, then so be it." Hardacre shrugged, reaching for a paper in his bureau drawer. "Here is a listing of the crew. I will have the purser supply you with names of the passengers. But when DuBois comes aboard at Cairo, you are to focus your attention on him. I want you to keep him in your sights at all times." He spoke these words with a finality that indicated that the interview was at an end.

"My wife wishes to send a post at our earliest docking. Do you have a typewriter aboard?"

"Yes. You will find one in the small mail room outside the pilots' quarters on the hurricane deck."

He took my hand and lightly pressed his lips to it. "I am sure you will find my boat most accommodating. It will be sometime tomorrow before we dock at Cairo and meet Mr. DuBois. I suggest you take full advantage of the many pleasures a riverboat affords."

I bowed my head slightly, then met his gaze straightforwardly. "Are you married, Mr. Hardacre?"

"No," he said with a smile, pushing his hand through

the waves of his hair. He was about to elaborate when a sharp rap fell on the stateroom door.

"I am sorry. Am I interrupting?"

"Not at all, Mr. Culbertson," said our host.

The same lanky fellow with the well-trimmed beard who had caused all the fuss on our departure stood at the partially opened door. His hands held several papers and a ledger book, while his face registered a look of surprise.

"My guests were just leaving." There was a silence, and when it became evident that no introductions were forthcoming from Mr. Hardacre, I intervened.

"We thoroughly enjoyed the most colorful manner by which you came aboard, Mr. Culbertson. I am Sadie Greenstreet, and this," I said with an indicating gesture, "is my husband Horace."

Mr. Culbertson looked disapprovingly at the wine glass I was still holding in my hand. "You are on holiday?"

I looked to Hardacre. "Mr. Greenstreet is a solicitor from Chicago, here to advise me on some business affairs."

The clerk gave us a forced smile. "I hope your stay is a pleasant one," he said.

"A riverboat has so much charm and romance, and if the others aboard are as interesting as the two we have met so far, I'm sure the trip will be most pleasant."

Hardacre stepped forward. "Well, I have a bit of business to take care of, and I am sure you wish to see your quarters. Stateroom C is the cabin just down the hall."

We took leave of our employer and his clerk and found our way to our stateroom door. The interior was much the same as Mr. Hardacre's, though much brighter and more cheery. It was a masculine cabin, decorated with pictures of sailing vessels and steamboats, maps, charts, and the like. A gimballed ship lantern hung from the ceiling, and sturdy walnut chairs were positioned in three of the corners. In the fourth stood a small writing desk.

To our right was an ornate highboy, complete with mirror. It held a porcelain pitcher and wash basin. The sleeping area was separated from the sitting area by chocolate-colored draw-string curtains. I drew them back and tried out the edge of the bed.

"I presume that bit of flirtation was in the line of duty," Horace said.

"Why, Horace," I said, with a significant smile, "I didn't believe you ever noticed such things."

"I notice," he said matter-of-factly. "I do not trust the man. What does your feminine intuition tell you about our employer?"

"He seemed straightforward enough, yet I could not help but feel he did not tell us all."

"My thoughts exactly. Why is he so cocksure he knows who has made the threats? His reasons are logical; still, you were right when you suggested that a man of his position is likely to have more than one enemy. And yet we are practically ordered to concentrate our attentions on this Mr. DuBois."

As he spoke, Horace removed a square of paper from his breast pocket. It contained no writing, but he pulled back the porthole curtains, attaching them to the swag,

then lifted the paper to the light. Next he pulled out another paper and compared the two. "These are very common papers, each without a watermark, and the very kind
a thousand people might possess. However," he said, "they
are similar." Now it was my turn to exhibit a blank look.
A moment later, the direction of his thoughts registered,
and I began to see where he was leading.

"He seems to have rather neat habits for a bachelor and
was educated at Eton," he continued. "If your observations are correct, neatness and educational polish are traits
of the author of this note."

"But, why would Mr. Hardacre fabricate a story, then
hire a Pinkerton to investigate it?"

"Why indeed?" Horace said, checking his silver pocket
watch. "It seems unlikely, but we must still consider it a
possibility. You will recall the case involving Mrs. Peters
of Gary, who hired a bodyguard for protection from her
husband. She cleverly gave the bodyguard the slip, killed
the husband, then claimed self-defense, stating at the in-
quest that her husband had threatened her. The fact that
she had hired a bodyguard nearly swayed the jury to think
in the way she had intended. But it is all idle speculation
at this point. I should like, however, to get a look at that
typewriter in the mail room. There is something about
Mr. Hardacre's story that doesn't ring true." He placed the
two papers in the desk. "There will be time enough to
think of our client and his case." His fingers played a mil-
itary drum roll on the porthole window ledge. He un-
clasped the rope on the window curtains and, smiling,
pulled the curtains shut.

V

A BLUE JAY'S
WARNING

The names of the river towns were exotic—Rome, Brandenburg, Cairo—romantic names which conjured up thoughts of excitement and intrigue. I had relayed these thoughts to Horace as I perused a map and itinerary on the train ride from Chicago. Horace had had an enigmatic smile on his face at the time, yet I had paid it no mind. Now I understood it. The towns were neither exotic nor romantic, nor their citizens intriguing. They were working towns just like a hundred others. All paid homage to the river, for it was their lifeblood; the wharf was the best-built and best-maintained structure in every town. Each community housed the same people, only with different faces, different names. There were hard-working roustabouts and wharf-hands with straw-bosses shouting orders in their ears and devil-may-care loafers, both black-skinned and white, sneering at the workers, yet envious of the jingle in their pockets. There were families, with only possessions enough to fill a small outhouse, waiting patiently at the wharf for a two-dollar packet. These people were willing to trade those romantically named towns for others with more modest names and, hopefully, better prospects.

Finally, there were the inevitable sharpers, fast-bloods, and gamblers, dressed in silk shirts and no suspenders, all with sleeves rolled up for an opportunity to exploit the others. And so, as we traveled further and further down

the Ohio, I became increasingly disappointed to hear the whistle sound the approach of the next town just round the bend. The river was magnificent, and the *Mississippi Girl* was truly a floating palace, but the towns with their misleading names were merely humdrum.

It was mid-afternoon now, some eight hours into our journey, and I was taking a stroll alone on the promenade deck, pondering over my observations. The weather was fair, and the south wind lazy. The pilot took us past the city of Rome, steering to leeward of a small island, keeping us close in and nearly under the shade of giant sycamores, where the only breeze was that afforded by the speed of the riverboat.

I was accosted presently by a man walking in the opposite direction. Accosted is the only word for it. He had just made an exit from the smoke-filled gambling hall, and, judging from the ruckus and catcalls that preceded him, there were more than a few who were happy to see him leave. He was in his later years, queer-looking, maypole thin, and appeared to possess all the nervous energy common to that sort. A prominent milk-white goatee jutted from his chin that reminded me of a snow-covered cattle-catcher on a C & O steam train. His eyebrows were the next feature to catch my eye. They were white, too, and stood out at odd angles as if charged with static electricity. His wallet was stuffed thickly with greenbacks, and he gave the leather a respectful caress before it disappeared into the lining of his top coat. The clothes on his back were all of the expensive sort, but some were old and some new, which seemed to suggest that his pocketbook and his luck were not always in the condition they were today. When he saw my face, his own brightened.

"I am Sidney Cotton, ship's doctor, at your service," he declared in a raspy voice. "And I must prescribe a turn or two around the hurricane deck." He offered me an arm. "It is heresy for a pretty woman to be strolling about by herself."

I eyed him suspiciously for a moment. At length, seeing he was perfectly earnest, and being beyond the age when one is offended by such liberties and straight talk, I took his arm.

"You are the second most beautiful lady aboard," he said with a wink as we stopped to look out from the bow.

"Second only?" I tried to sound hurt.

He patted his breast pocket. "I've been staring straight into the face of a lady named luck for the last three hours. Why, just five minutes ago, she handed me a pair of handsome red jacks to keep company with the two black ones I was already holding." The old man spat a tobacco plug over the railing, and we watched it sail into a metal bucket on the deck below. The feat seemed to give him as much pleasure as his winning at cards.

"I shouldn't think a riverboat would have its own doctor. Is there really enough illness to keep you busy?"

"Well, I guess you're right, Miss . . . I don't believe I caught the name."

"Sadie Greenstreet," I said, "and it is Mrs."

He tipped an imaginary hat. "There's no denying it. I get scarce little work on the *Mississippi Girl* outside of the occasional hangover or putting a little plaster to the face of a crew member when he gets into a scrape."

I began to sense he might be threading a yarn about being a medical man. "Then why do you choose to practice aboard a riverboat?" I asked, giving him an oblique look.

"We all have our little vices, Mrs. Greenstreet," he said, whittling off a new plug of tobacco with what looked like a scalpel. Maybe he *was* a doctor, I thought. "Mine happens to be gambling. I'd been retired for nigh on three years when the missus died. I took to traveling on the riverboats. By and by I struck a deal with Mr. Hardacre, owner of this here showboat. Mr. Hardacre thought it would be a fine thing to have his own doctor aboard and . . ." he said, shrugging his shoulders and raising a shaggy brow. "I figured it would be an even trade for being so close to the gambling saloon."

The *Mississippi Girl* moved downriver at a surprisingly leisurely pace. While our talk drifted into various channels, more than once we were passed by boats half our size. When a two-man skiff weighed down with cotton bales as high as its mast flag came chugging by, leaving only the sting of a shrill whistle ringing in my ear, I felt obliged to inquire.

"Why are we traveling so slowly, Dr. Cotton? The current is strongest in the middle of the river. Shouldn't we be traveling there?

"What is the purpose of a showboat?" my companion said with the voice of a philosopher.

"I always imagined it was to get people from here to there in style."

"That's about an eighth of it," he said, trying to be exact. "The other seven-eighths has to do with making money." He pointed to the gambling saloon. "A considerable amount is passed around between those four walls, and I suspect an equal amount is spilled on the parquet. And, that's not to mention the platoon of professional ladies who earn more in a day than a doctor does in a week. So, if it takes a day or two longer to reach St. Louis, well, I guess the captain and Mr. Hardacre won't be complaining." The old doctor sent another missile on its way toward the steerage deck. "Is your husband aboard?"

"Yes. He's gone below to visit the barber and to post a letter. He promised to meet me within the hour."

We passed a crossing near the timber-laden river bank when Dr. Cotton cupped a hand to his ear. "Listen," he said earnestly.

Over the incessant hum of the engines, I could hear only the vague squawkings of birds in the nearby trees.

"It's the blue jays. They're crying out 'thief, thief!' Listen," he said again. "There's an old story in this here part of the country that says the blue jay knows a man's heart, and whenever he makes his warning cry you'd better hold on tight to your purse because someone's planning to steal it."

"Well, just maybe," I said, "it's a warning to the men at the gambling tables to guard against a certain grey-haired doctor who has plans for their money."

Dr. Cotton smiled broadly as the alluring and melodic pipings of a steam calliope made its way from the gambling room. "Would you care to watch the game or try your own hand at the table?"

"Perhaps some other time. But you go on. My husband should be here shortly. Good luck," I said as he turned to go. Another jay gave its call, and Dr. Sidney Cotton sent a roguish wink in my direction, then disappeared into the saloon.

"It is, at the very least, a curious coincidence, Sadie,"

said a familiar voice from behind. I turned to find Horace. His boots had recently seen the hand of a bootblack, the brown felt derby in his hand was newly brushed, and his hair was neatly trimmed and lacquered with a lemon creme.

"What is, at least, a curious coincidence?" I asked.

"I have been to the mail room, and the typewriter there was manufactured by Sholes and Company of Milwaukee. I typed out the series of letters just as you suggested. It was all I could do to keep my motives from the purser, who seems to think looking over the passengers' shoulders is among his duties." He handed me the paper. The letters H, I, T and R appeared to correspond with those on the threatening note.

"I also found out a thing or two while in the barber's chair. A well-tipped barber can be a valuable ally, Sadie. If he can be believed, Captain McQuaid has had a running feud with Mr. Hardacre for the last six months. McQuaid was fired in Cincinnati, but, when Hardacre couldn't find a replacement, he agreed that the captain should keep his berth for one final run. There are regulations against putting out a steamship without a certified captain; otherwise, the *Mississippi Girl* would have shipped out without him. And, I got the distinct impression that McQuaid was more upset over the loss of his command than Hardacre let on to us." Horace drew forth his pocket note pad. "There is another man aboard who may have his finger in the case—a Dr. Sidney Cotton."

I looked at Horace with surprise. "I was just talking to the man. He's a very engaging, elderly gentleman."

"He is also in substantial debt to Mr. Hardacre—debts incurred in the gambling saloon."

"Well, he's doing better today," I said and, as I spoke, I noticed Horace's eyes roaming the steerage deck below. A young couple stood very near each other, their eyes searching the steerage deck with the air of spies. The man's collar was turned up, and his hat pulled down in the conspiratorial manner of a secret agent. Indeed, if the war had not been eight years over, I do believe my imagination would have made the couple such. There was something disturbingly familiar about the two. She was a light-haired woman, simply dressed in a plain flower-patterned dress that, nonetheless, showed to her advantage a remarkable figure. He was of modest height, yet stood erect and proud despite the patches on either elbow of his jacket. A cigarette hung below his well-trimmed brown moustache. They spoke urgently to each other, he gesticulating with his hand, she mostly listening with a worried look on her face. Their disagreement, if that is what it was, turned out to be slight, for they embraced warmly, then stood gazing out onto the river scenery. We never spoke of the young couple till some time later, yet, I could see on Horace's features that they had produced a profound effect.

Horace gave his chin a contemplative tug before turning toward me. "Shall we test our theory and compare these newly typed letters with the note in our cabin? If they prove to be from the same typewriter, we can assume that whoever wrote the threatening note to Mr. Hardacre is aboard the *Mississippi Girl* this very moment."

We returned to our stateroom. Just as Horace's hand prepared to turn the key, our attentions were diverted to a flurry and row within the quarters of Elcid Hardacre.

A lattice-work transom window was partially open, emitting a thick, deep voice which slurred out an oath and epithets at Hardacre. I heard a sound, presumably of a fist slamming against a table.

"No, sir. I won't take a seat. I won't be taking orders from the likes of you."

Hardacre answered the man calmly but with emphasis on each word. "You are a fool. A drunken fool, if I'm not mistaken. Let me remind you that my say-so carries a fair amount of weight on the river. If you value your livelihood, you should have a care before I decide to make an example of you. A blacklisted captain will never find work on this man's river."

"I'll show you whether I'm a fool, and I'll show you whether I'm drunk."

I expected blows to follow, but instead a large man in a disheveled maritime uniform, with a wild eye and surly countenance, pushed through the door, slamming it closed. His mottled face possessed a stubble of hair as unkempt and uneven as a newly threshed wheat field. "You haven't heard the end of this, mister," he shouted to the closed door, "not by a long shot!" He gave a start and grunted upon seeing he was not alone in the hallway. He wore a five-button waistcoat and fumbled with the third button for a second or two but, having no success in putting it through the matching button hole, gave it up. Swinging around, he began careening from one wall to the other. In a moment, he had disappeared, leaving behind only the pungent fragrance of distilled juniper berries.

"I believe we have just made the acquaintance of Captain McQuaid," Horace said. He stood unmoving for an instant, as if deciding whether to pay Mr. Hardacre another visit, then returned to the door lock. As our stateroom door swung open, Horace almost at once screwed up his face. He raised his right hand, bidding me to stay put as his eyes wandered high and low around the room. After crossing the room and pulling the curtains open, he began pacing the room, first in straight lines, then in counter-clockwise circles, as if taking its measure. In the next minutes, he sniffed and poked about the cabin, stalking it like a man on the borders of lunacy. He looked in the closet, the dresser, and under the bed. "Damn," he muttered under his breath when he turned his attention to the desk drawers, searching through them thoroughly. As his hand reached for the candle stand and touched the wax, I saw at last the explanation for his actions. When we had left the compartment, there had been a new taper candle in the holder. I had placed it there myself. The one I was now staring at had been lit and burned down a good half an inch.

"The wax is cold," Horace said. "The thief is gone."

"Thief?" I repeated, remembering Dr. Cotton's story.

"The note to Mr. Hardacre is missing. And so are several agency papers. Whoever was here now knows I am a Pinkerton and why I was engaged."

"What are you going to do?" I inquired.

"For one thing, I will make certain that if this happens again, we will be prepared." Pulling a small metal box from his travel satchel, he extracted a small tube of white powder from among other vials, keys, and implements of his trade and began to sprinkle the white substance near the door. "Be careful not to step just there," he said, returning the half-empty container to its previous residence. "Fuller's earth adheres well to an oiled shoe. If the intruder returns, we will know who it is by the mark this powder leaves on his shoe. A criminal will sometimes return to the place of a crime, Sadie, although in this case, the thief probably has what he wants. It is unlikely we shall have further uninvited visitors."

Horace spent the twilight hours in quiet reflection, smoking one after another of his misshapen cigarettes. He had another brief visit with Elcid Hardacre, but did not mention the missing papers.

I consciously forced myself away from my stateroom and my book and took a turn around the walkway that looked down on the grand saloon. With the help of Dr. Cotton and the roulette table, I even managed to parlay twenty dollars of Pinkerton money into thirty of my own. But I returned to the cabin early, feeling a pang of guilt for enjoying myself while Horace worried over the case.

While the music from a duet of mosquitoes kept me wide-eyed until midnight or beyond, thoughts buzzed in and out of my brain. Who was it that had entered our cabin, stealing only the note to Mr. Hardacre and some

Pinkerton papers? Could it be the captain, trying to throw a scare into the man who had fired him? Or was it someone else aboard—the clerk named Culbertson, or even Dr. Cotton? Surely not Dr. Cotton. It might be as Hardacre concluded—that the source of the threat was the rival steamboat owner named DuBois. Yet that seemed less likely now than it had, unless DuBois possessed an ally aboard the boat. Perhaps, as Horace had suggested, this was all an elaborate scheme by Hardacre himself in which we were being used. But to what end?

"Keep your eyes and ears open, Sadie," Horace had advised earlier. "There is danger here. I can feel it. It may come from Mr. DuBois or from some other quarters; but, rest assured, it will come. Working on a case has much in common with working on a picture puzzle, Sadie. But it is often more difficult; we are not only given a small number of the pieces, but only have a vague notion what the picture should look like in the end."

The face of my husband looked strange and unfamiliar that night. But it was not the yellow candlelight nor the drops of laudanum which made it so. It was something else, something intangible. At last, I realized what it was. The man who paced the room was not the man I married. He had grown old with the grace with which a confident man grows old. Lines of character intersected his face. Some, I knew, were caused by worry over me.

I wanted to get up from that bed and look at my own face and eyes to see if they had fared as well. But I knew the answer. "Goodnight, Sadie," I heard him say.

Unwilling sleep came at last, and so came dreams—dreams of Elcid Hardacre standing in a circle with a black-bird on his shoulder while Captain McQuaid, Dr. Cotton, Mr. Culbertson, and others whose faces I could not discern danced round and round him.

VI

Tragedy on the Ohio

The Ohio has many moods. There are eerie mornings when fog hangs low and giant elm trees glower oppressively over the steamboat. At these times, the pilot steers slowly, carefully, as if trying to steal his way without disturbing Nature. In contrast, there are brilliant, sunlit moments when the steamer finds itself in water as wide and clear as a crystal-studded lake. The pilot then cries, "No bottom ahead!" and we fairly dance and glide across the silvery water without a care.

The river was in the former mood, its mood of mystery, on the second day out. The morning was cool, and we woke to witness a foreboding fog hanging about the boat like an unearthly shroud. Several passengers had braved the promenade deck, cautiously clutching the railing. Some marveled out loud at the skill of the pilot. We had been slowed to a crawl, yet even that was a remarkable feat in those conditions. "Are we heading down river or straight for shore?" I heard someone inquire. "Will we strike a hidden shoal or some unseen barge or flatboat?" wondered another. Was there even a body up there manning the pilot's chair? Who could tell? We all just looked about in astonishment and imagined the man in the wheel-house, decked in his brass-buttoned suit, gently rocking the great steering wheel and calmly staring into the misty nature like some mythic hero.

By and by, the fog lifted slightly, which afforded us a view of at least the passengers on the deck below. The mysterious woman and her patch-elbowed companion

stood on the port side. Their figures appeared and disappeared, then appeared again, as the riverboat passed through varying degrees of cool vapor. They were speaking to each other in an earnest, almost argumentative manner, just as they had been the day before. Something shiny was passed from his hand to hers, and was exchanged for a carpetbag the size of a large melon. The shiny object might have been a watch, but I could not be sure. The man with the moustache looked up and, seeing us, hooked the woman's arm and walked away from the bow.

"An interesting couple; what do you make of them, Sadie?"

"They are familiar, yet I can't place them. Have we met them before?"

Horace smiled, but, before he could answer, a voice hailed us from behind.

"Hello there," called the venerable voice of Dr. Cotton. He took off a wide-brimmed straw hat and waved it at the fog as one waves at a pesky fly. "It's as thick as Indian pudding out here," he said.

He looked much the same as he had the day before, except for that fine straw hat, which he returned, slightly off plumb, to his head. Introductions and good mornings were passed around.

"Cigar?" asked the doctor, producing a pair of eight-inch cheroots from his vest pocket.

Horace accepted, squinting down the long cigar as one sights a rifle barrel. "Brazilian cigars are a scarce commodity," Horace said, while cutting off one end with a pen knife.

The old doctor's grey-green eyes twinkled. "The captain has connections with a Louisiana clipper that trades in sugar and tobacco."

"Captain McQuaid?"

Dr. Cotton hesitated. "Yes, McQuaid. I take it you've met."

"In a manner of speaking. But I don't think he would remember us."

"Too bad about McQuaid, too bad. He's a good man, not the kind to be drinking while at the command. But the man is a relic of the past, just like me, and I guess things just got to him." Dr. Cotton puffed at his cheroot, watching the smoke rise and mingle with the fog. "These days, the two pilots run the boat, and with Mr. Hardacre aboard making all the decisions, there's not much to do for a Captain used to giving orders, not taking them."

"I understand he is about to be leaving?" I asked.

Dr. Cotton nodded. "It was six months ago and on our very first voyage that we had an encounter with a steamship named the *Natchez*. She was a cargo steamer with a reputation as the fastest on the Mississippi." The doctor rolled his cigar to the other side of his mouth and continued. "We were heading down river some six miles up from Memphis when we heard the four whistles that signified she was under full steam and ready to pass us by. Mr. Hardacre comes on deck just about then and tells the boys there's an extra day's wages for them if we are the first to dock in Memphis.

"Well, we held our own till we were within a mile of the city, when Captain McQuaid went below to check our pressure and ordered the firemen to quit shoveling. McQuaid had seen too many races turn to disaster when an over-heated boiler blew a boat clear out of the water. The *Natchez* passed us by, so close you could hear the raillery and ridicule of her crew. Hardacre went into a rage, and the two have been feuding ever since.

"But I suspect there's another reason, too," he continued. "A young buck just finished with an apprenticeship will hire on for two or three hundred dollars a month. McQuaid, on the other hand, has been running the rivers for some twenty years and won't work for less than five."

"I hope Hardacre isn't too hard to work for," I said with a laugh. "Horace is his newly hired solicitor."

"Well, that is a pleasant surprise," Dr. Cotton said, while looking at me. "Then you'll be with us for more than just the trip to St. Louis?"

"That matter has not yet been settled," said Horace. He contemplated his cigar for a long moment while he considered his next words. "I have been left to my own devices to learn about the management of the boat before I make recommendations for improvements," he continued. "Perhaps you could furnish me with some information."

"My pleasure," rejoined the good-humored doctor.

"Who are the occupants of the first-class berths?"

"Well, let me see. Down the end of the hall is Mr. Hardacre, and across from him is the purser, Mr. Culbertson. The two near rooms are Captain McQuaid's and my own. There are two rooms between Culbertson and myself which I believe are to be filled by passengers boarding at Cairo."

"And, we have the room next to Captain McQuaid," I said. "What of the compartment between us and Hardacre?"

Dr. Cotton tugged at his pointed beard. "That room is connected to Mr. Hardacre's stateroom. Let me put it this way. Elcid Hardacre is a bachelor. Need I say more?"

Our conversation was interrupted as a splash of water

preceded the shrill cry of a woman. We all turned in the direction of the steerage deck below.

"My God, someone has fallen in," the doctor said softly, as if to himself. Then, throwing his two-dollar cheroot over the rail, he repeated his words, this time shouting up to the pilothouse. We leaned over the railing and saw the woman in the flower-print dress standing alone on the lower deck.

At once, a young cub pilot came on a run, bawling orders and generally taking charge. "Down the larboard skiff! I need four oarsmen. Higgins and Irish Tom. Fetch a rope there, Saunders! Hurry on now, Billy," he shouted. "Stop the engines!"

Before the commands could be turned into actions, two faint, muffled cries rang out, though in which direction none could tell. From the stern, a resounding thud rocked the boat as if something hard had crashed into the paddle wheel. The engines were halted, and the woman below gave out another terrible cry that echoed in the surrounding wood; when it faded, all that remained was the thin whistle of steam escaping from the boiler room. Everyone stood stock still for an instant. I had heard that sickening sound from the wheel once before, when the steamer had rolled over an unseen snag. But today, it could only mean one thing.

The pilot's apprentice and his crew of oarsmen set down their skiff and began to row to and fro while the passengers gathered on the lower deck and looked helplessly on. Horace betrayed little reaction to the young man's fate.

Perhaps that's just the casehardened way of a Pinkerton. Horace had investigated and probed into more than a few killings, and had seen his share of death and suffering from natural causes. In the line of duty, he'd even been a party to one or two men's end. Yet I was surprised and just a bit disappointed when Horace showed such little com-

passion for the young widow. He finished his cigar, rolled up a particularly fat cigarette, and stood gazing laconically out into the hazy sky. "Shall we go below to get a better look?" he said.

The moments followed each other in slow procession. An hour passed, then two. With each passing moment, so went any vestige of lingering hope. At times, a flurry of useless activity would break out when someone would dash for a bulls-eye lantern or a length of hemp rope, then the dead silence of waiting would set in again. Near the bow, a pitch-pine torch did little to break through the fog. Whispered comments identifying the couple as newlyweds made their way from one ear to the next, making the tragedy all the more melancholy.

Floating near the boat, the man's tall hat was all that

was found, and, when the sad-faced widow, with eyes as red and puffy as a bee sting, held it in her hands, the passengers and crew alike began filing by her, filling it with what they could afford. By the time Dr. Cotton began escorting the teary-eyed woman to her berth, the hat was brimming with greenbacks and silver.

"Horace!" I said, admonishingly. "Are you not going to help that poor woman?" Horace looked over the rail, his eyes still searching.

"How much do you suggest I give?" he returned in an irreverent manner I found almost offensive.

"If you do not put five dollars in that hat, you shall find yourself sleeping on the steerage deck bunks instead of in compartment C."

"You are probably right." Horace shrugged. "Excuse me, ma'am," he said, touching the woman's elbow. Wide orphan eyes looked out from beneath a calosh hood. "My wife insisted that you have this." With a grandiloquent bow, he slipped a five-dollar note into the black hat.

"If there is anything my wife or I can do, please do not hesitate to ask." After writing a brief message on the backside, he handed her his card.

The woman stared confusedly at him, looking as if she would faint. It may have been the way the sun had broken through the fog just then—but I thought I read fear on the woman's face. Horace showed no sign of emotion.

"Thank . . . thank you, sir," she said haltingly, and Dr. Cotton escorted her away.

VII

RESURRECTION
IN CAIRO

A h! I see we are taking on three new passengers,"
Horace said when our boat had docked in Cairo.
"I'm sure one of them is the man we have been hired to
protect Mr. Hardacre against." Horace looked beyond to
the elbow of land locked between the clear Ohio and the
muddy Mississippi.

The word "Cairo" was painted in green on a clapboard
that swung from iron chains between two high poles on the
wharf. Beyond was a little town—not the sleepy, un-
eventful kind I had written about in my diary the day before, but a bustling town, all decked out in banners of red,
white, and blue which served a reminder that today was
Independence Day. Houses, set haphazardly here and
there, were at odds with a perfectly straight high street
which reached nearly a quarter mile from the river. Boardwalks lined the street, with here and there a horse tied up
to a hitch pole.

Up the hill walked that pathetic young widow whose
husband had met such a deadly end. The local police had
come aboard and made inquiries, promising to send a
search party back upriver to look for the body. The

woman, on her part, braved her ill-starred fate with uncommon steadfastness. She said there were people in town
she knew, and she insisted on going alone to find them.

Her pace increased as she walked away from the
wharf, and, as her pace quickened, she began looking fran-

tically from side-to-side. From an alleyway, a man emerged
and shadowed the woman for several steps.

Without breath, I followed her steps as the man closed
in on her, grabbing her at last from behind. A passerby,
leading an old brindled horse, ambled by them, yet didn't
bother to stop or even take notice. First the loss of her husband and now this. What an unmerciful world, I thought.

The man swung her around in a wide circle before releasing her. When her feet touched the ground, she turned to face the man, then made a quick move to her fallen travelling satchel. Pulling out a black top hat, she showed him the contents. She pointed toward our steamboat and, at that moment, I noticed the man's jacket was patched at the elbows. He turned to look at the *Mississippi Girl,* and I then recognized the man's thin moustache with a cigarette tucked under it—and at last knew who that couple reminded me of.

"They do look uncommonly familiar," Horace said as we watched the couple embrace. "Are you still angry that I only gave them five dollars?"

"I think they probably earned it." I sent back his smile, and, as I did, I lost my thoughts for some moments, remembering twenty years ago, and a hundred of our own little escapades and schemes.

"How did you know?" I said, when the present had returned.

"When I came back from the barber yesterday, I first noticed the pair. I see now that they were in the midst of their preparations. The man had pointed to a small carpetsack, which he held in one hand, then made a gesture toward the paddle wheel. I would have not given the matter a second thought, had I not looked more closely at the carpetbag. It contained an object which was too large for the bag and was sticking out at the side of the flap. It was a log, Sadie. A common fireplace log."

"A log? That is unusual."

"Exactly my thoughts, and, when I casually strolled by, they eyed me suspiciously and walked the other way."

"So, today," I said, "he used the log for flotation when he jumped in the water, then tossed it against the paddle-wheel to make us all believe he had been struck. Quite a daring bit of play acting."

"Admirable on her part also, though I did detect the faint odor of ammonia spirits when I spoke with her and gave her my card. She must have had it in her handker-chief, and it produced the appropriate tears and redness when she put the handkerchief to her eyes."

"Why did you give her your card?" I asked. "And what did you write on it?"

"I couldn't resist letting her know that I had seen through their foolproof scheme. I handed her my Pinker-ton card on which I offered congratulations for their well-planned enterprise."

Horace's left hand rested on his forehead, shading his eyes from the late afternoon sun. He held the position for some moments, calling to mind a saluting soldier. There was a touch of reverence in the pose that made me won-der if it were not indeed a salute—a salute to the ingenu-ity of the two social bandits, a salute to their youth, their energy. Perhaps even a salute to our own youth.

The pair stood near a white-washed church. It domi-nated the Cairo landscape, its spire reaching to the sky like an exclamation point. In front of the church's red brick stairs, which led to open front doors, a one-legged man, probably a war veteran, leaned on a Y-shaped tree branch. By his feet was a tin cup and in one hand he held another, this one filled with stick matches or lead pencils.

The woman reached into her bag and placed something in the beggar's tin cup. Horace's hand came down from his forehead. Somewhere a bell tolled five times. The profiteers slipped down a nearby alleyway, disappearing from our line of view and our lives.

"There is just one thing I do not understand."

"What is that?"

"How did

he get to Cairo ahead of us?"

"That is a mystery," Horace said, laughing. "But, I think it's only right that we don't uncover the truth of all their secrets."

"Mystery is the antagonist of truth. It is a fog of human invention that obscures truth and represents it in distortion," I reflected.

"Your esteemed old Tom Paine," said Horace matter-of-factly. "But I don't believe he was referring to this kind of mystery."

I shook my head, surprised. "Horace, you never cease to amaze."

VIII

MISSISSIPPI WATER

A bright summer sun and a showboat is a combination that will withstand even the gloom of tragedy. One by one the cargo of pleasure seekers began doing their best to forget the events of the day. Ladies in pastel crinolines, armed with like-colored parasols, reclaimed the boat's lower decks, strolling, admiring the white gloves on their fingers, lounging on deck chairs, or merely idly chatting with one another. Meanwhile, a medley of Stephen Foster tunes, smoke, and laughter issued forth from the saloon.

The first of three Cairo newcomers, a young woman in silver-rimmed spectacles and a broad-brimmed hat, passed us by on her way to the texas. The hat was stylish, a gauzy summer bonnet with untied lavender strings hanging from either side of her face. Finding no fault in her head dress, I was forced to look elsewhere. Her hair was a pale yellow, the result of a rinse I calculated, noting her eyebrows were several shades darker. Not a man aboard would notice such a thing, I was quite sure, but to me it stood out like a fly on white wallpaper. She wore a grey quarter-length cape about her shoulders despite the July sun. "I understand there is a doctor aboard," she said to the man carrying her bags.

"Yes ma'am. That would be Dr. Cotton."

"I may have to stop by his room after I'm settled. I am afraid I get a bit light-headed whenever my feet leave solid ground."

"Dr. Cotton has a room just two doors down from you," the attendant said.

Their voices moved beyond earshot up the staircase but were replaced by others.

"Mr. Greenstreet," one of them called. It was the ship's clerk, Mr. Culbertson, and with him were a man and woman, each on the outer borders of middle age. Culbertson motioned us to join them. A red finger sign, on which was written the word "Saloon", pointed to a pair of swinging doors, and the party of three disappeared behind them.

"If I am correct," Horace said, "that is Andrew DuBois. Assuming that is his wife," he continued, "and assuming DuBois is a sensible man, it is a good sign that he brought her along."

I gave Horace a questioning look.

"A sensible man does not bring along his wife if there is danger in his mission." He gave me a significant glance.

"It is often the case when comparing a husband and wife, that the wife is the more formidable of the two," I said.

Horace pulled at his side whiskers. "At any rate, Sadie, there lies our duty," Horace said, pointing toward the saloon. "I would have much preferred following my own lines, but since Mr. Hardacre insists we not let DuBois out of our sights, we must follow our client's wishes. I was not able to convince him that danger may come from other quarters than DuBois, but at least he was agreeable to keeping himself locked in his room until his meeting with DuBois."

We entered the saloon and looked about the crowded room. Mr. Culbertson and his two companions were settling

down to a corner table, the only quiet corner in the entire saloon. It was a very showy saloon. Hanging from the ceiling, and surrounded by a promenade walkway, were rimed chandeliers. A fair-haired young lady in a gossamer silk gown performed on a small stage. No one seemed to mind in the least that her sultry rendering of "Camptown Races" bore little resemblance to Foster's tune. She wore green gloves, so green they might have disappeared if left lying on the billiard table behind her. She stretched them toward her audience on reaching the final note.

The bar was brass-railed and long, stretching nearly the length of the near wall. Three white-frocked bartenders with sleeves rolled to the elbows manned the bar. With ironic grins, they dispensed liquid good cheer from varnished casks and from bottles. The patrons in this room could be called society's lucky ones, the ones who could afford to take their doses of happiness in such a place as this. I compared their expressions to the faces of the family on the dock at Rome who waited for a cheap packet and passage to a new life. It seemed to me that family possessed a quiet hopefulness absent in this room.

To the left were gaming tables—poker, roulette, and red-dog. I searched the tables for a white goatee amongst the players and was disappointed when I saw none. All four walls were decorated with fretwork and mirrors, which had the effect of multiplying the room many times over. A working girl, whose flouncy white muslin dress was in sharp contrast with her mulatto skin, gave Horace a flirtatious wink, but before his imagination could take hold, I took his arm and led him to the table where Culbertson was seated with his two guests. He addressed us in a cool, businesslike manner.

"Andrew DuBois, Mrs. DuBois, this is Mr. Hardacre's new solicitor, Horace Greenstreet, and his wife, Sadie."

Horace shook hands with Andrew DuBois, a stocky man with diagonal lines radiating from the corners of his mouth at unequal angles like a badly mitred picture frame. An insufficient head of hair was accentuated by two tufts, one at ten o'clock and one at two, each serving to further punctuate the squareness of his head. He wore a grey jacket, which protruded slightly near the place of his breast pocket. It was a revolver-sized protrusion.

I took a seat next to Mrs. DuBois and regarded her briefly. She was dark-haired but otherwise nondescript, like a hundred other faces one might see walking down Chicago's Broadway on a Saturday night. Her two most prominent features were not really features at all—a grotesquely large and heavily jeweled ring that was worn like a badge of success on her little finger, and the pungent odor of jasmine. She wore no hat.

She seemed to be studying me just as I studied her; it was not a woman's glance, but straightforward, more like a man's, or like sister Pamela staring at me, trying to read my thoughts. At length, she gave me a brief Queen-of-England smile.

"You mentioned entertainment?" Horace said, noticing the singer had left the stage.

"Yes, I suspect the entertainment will begin any moment—ah, it won't be long now," Culbertson said, as outside the boat's whistle blew twice. I could feel we were slipping away from the Cairo dock. "Mr. Hardacre has ordered us to stay in Cairo until midnight," he continued, ignoring the fact we were moving. "There will be the Cairo fireworks on shore and a celebration on board, which will begin momentarily." He turned to DuBois. "Mr. Hardacre will see you at nine o'clock, to entertain your proposal, though I don't see the point of it all. He has no intentions of selling the *Mississippi Girl.*"

"Don't be so sure, now. The whole world is for sale at the right price. Isn't that right, Mr. Greenstreet?"

"There are certain things which cannot be bought with money."

"Such idealistic talk for a lawyer," DuBois said. "I've seen men who would sell their souls for a glass of cheap whiskey." My foot searched under the table for Horace's foot and when I found it, I placed mine on top of his. Unfortunately, this did not produce any effect, as he continued to study Mr. DuBois. Mrs. DuBois, however, stared at me with wide eyes. I blushed, removed my foot, and returned her look with my own queenly smile.

Horace pulled out his smoking gear. "I've always been a freethinker, Mr. DuBois, so a glass of whiskey seems a fair enough price to me, as long as it's not cheap whiskey."

DuBois slapped his hand on the table with a congenial laugh as he watched Horace's right hand manipulate a cigarette. "I like you, Greenstreet." Then, to the serving girl, "Bring us a bottle of your best bourbon."

Some ten minutes passed since the boat had slipped away from shore. Captain McQuaid entered the saloon presently, flanked by crewmen on each side, all with tin growlers in hand. After setting the buckets on the bar, the captain turned and cleared his throat loudly to gain attention. He was in much finer condition than the day before, well-shaven, with only a bit of redness about the eyes to betray his former state. He patiently cleaned a clay cutty pipe with a long iron nail while the bar keepers and serving girls busied themselves by filling glasses with a grey-brown liquid from the buckets, placing one glass before everyone in the room.

"This is the entertainment I spoke of," said Culbertson.

As glasses were passed around, some looked on in inquiring anticipation while others wore knowing smiles on their faces. Dr. Cotton entered the room, tipping a phantom hat to the young girl who supplied him with a glass. He spoke briefly to McQuaid before taking his customary place amongst the gamblers.

We were the last to be served, and I examined the murky contents with astonishment. It contained all manner of debris—floating foam, brown silty material which was sinking to the bottom, and suspended grey and green flecks moving about as if alive.

Captain McQuaid stood in the center of the great room. "We have reached the Mississippi," he announced in his deep-voiced manner. A few passengers apparently familiar with the ceremony gave out shouts of approval.

The words McQuaid then delivered were measured and exact, as if they had been given many times before; they had the force and sureness of a well-worn pulpit sermon imparted by a fire and brimstone rector.

"They say a thimbleful of Mississippi water will sustain a man for a day, a glassful for a week. The water in these glasses come from all parts of this great country, from the hills of Pennsylvania clear over to the Dakota Territories. The Indians call it the Father of Waters. To my way of thinking, they got it wrong. The Mississippi is more like a lady. Now, she has a few affairs on her way down, with

the St. Croix, the Wisconsin, and the like. And a tumultuous fling with the Missouri a few hundred miles north of here. But when she marries up with the Ohio, that's when she takes on her special properties."

Captain McQuaid doffed his hat with the left hand while lifting his glass high in the air with the right. "This will be my last voyage on the *Mississippi Girl*. To your health," he said, bringing the glass to his lips. He looked about the room slowly as if taking it in one final time. "We'll be returning you to the Cairo wharf now."

About half the passengers drained their glasses with the Captain. Others did so reluctantly, at the prodding of their neighbors. Mr. DuBois poured a small amount of bourbon into our glasses. "That should take care of anything still alive," he said, and we each in turn followed the captain's toast. The piano player struck up a tune, while outside, Fourth of July revelers began shooting off firecrackers and their guns into the air.

"Quite a little ceremony," Horace said, striking up a conversation with Culbertson. "A tradition, I take it."

Culbertson nodded. "That was a much abridged version. He usually rambles on for fifteen minutes or more. I would not be surprised if he's beginning to believe in the yarns he tells."

"Did I hear correctly?" asked DuBois. "This is to be his last command? He looks too young for a retirement."

"He lost his berth due to a disagreement with Mr. Hardacre," explained Culbertson. "But I'm sure he will have no trouble securing another."

"I could use a man like that running one of my boats." DuBois appeared to be contemplating his own suggestion, for he toyed with his glass for a few seconds without speaking. "Excuse me a moment," he said, then walked over to the captain, shaking his right hand vigorously, while pressing what appeared to be a business card in the other.

"Why such an interest in the *Mississippi Girl?*" Horace asked, when the businessman returned. "Surely there must be other showboats with owners more willing to negotiate a sale."

DuBois poured more bourbon. "None like the *Mississippi Girl.* She has a reputation. Just look around you, Greenstreet. There isn't a riverboat like her in the world. I was forced into this business by the railroads. No one ships by riverboat anymore. But people will always want to travel—and to gamble. All of my showboats are made-over freighters, and they all lack style. I like to do everything with style."

"Why not build your own?"

"That would take eighteen months at best," DuBois said, and, as he spoke, I studied the deep mitred lines on his face and his furrowed brow. They were hard lines, and it struck me he was a hard man, used to getting his way. Ironically, he very much reminded me of Hardacre. Perhaps it was the way of all riverboat owners, I thought.

"At this point in my life," DuBois continued, "I figure it's better to get things done today. There may not be a tomorrow." He was looking straight at Horace.

IX

Murder in Stateroom G

It was nearly quarter past eight o'clock. Andrew DuBois had nearly single-handedly kept the conversation alive during a long dinner with a succession of anecdotal stories, most having something to do with his past business dealings. Only once, when I became aware of Mrs. DuBois' steady gaze, was I called upon to speak at any length.

"Your face is quite familiar, Mrs. Greenstreet. I don't mean like someone I've seen a long time ago, but more like someone I've seen many times. You say you are from Chicago?"

"We are."

She shook her head. "That is strange, because I never forget a face, yet we rarely visit Chicago."

There were reasons, I thought, for Horace to take on the role of a lawyer, but none for me to conceal my own work. Besides, the woman might remember me at any moment. "Do you ever read the *Chicago Tribune?*" I asked.

She cupped her palms together, eyes widening. "Of course. I've never seen your face before but I do see your likeness next to your advice column every Sunday evening."

"What kind of advice do you give?" asked her husband.

"I answer my readers' questions. Mostly practical, common-sense advice—everything from how to remove ink stains from trousers to how to keep husbands from the red light district."

Mrs. DuBois's eyes raised as if to say, "Perhaps you could enlighten me on the latter."

I was relieved when Horace changed the subject. "I understand you recently purchased a steamer called the *Prairie Clipper*." Horace gave Mr. DuBois a look that communicated the intent of his question.

Straightening himself in his cane back chair, he answered, "I know what they say about that business. They say I had a hand in the accident. I hear the whispers. But let me tell you, Mr. Greenstreet, I am a man of honor. I usually get what I want, but I do so in an honorable way."

For some reason, the words of Emerson came to mind: "The louder he talked of his honor, the faster we counted our spoons." Yet the man did seem in earnest. I have found, through the years, that the more successful a man is, the harder he is to read. And this was certainly the case with Andrew DuBois.

I rubbed the back of the green cat's-eye pendant that always hangs from my neck. It was my mother's and since her death when I was ten years old I have never taken it off. Whenever I find myself agitated, worried, or in deep thought I rub its smooth polished surface, and nine times out of ten it calms me or helps me think through a problem.

Maybe Hardacre had read him wrong. If DuBois was, as he said, an honorable man, then Hardacre was wrong and Horace was protecting him against the wrong man.

Discomforted, I stared at the chandelier hanging at the center of the saloon. It looked icy cold, like the hoarfrost in my garden on a winter morning. Maybe it was the thought of cold, maybe it was the bourbon, or maybe it was the unshakable notion that something tragic was soon to come that made me shiver.

The voice of Allan Culbertson interrupted my thoughts. "You will have to excuse me," he said, rising from his chair. "I must make some arrangements for your meeting with Mr. Hardacre. I will send someone when he is ready. You will find Mr. Hardacre is a very punctual man." He checked his pocket watch. "It is now eight-fifty. We will be down at nine o'clock. I'm sure Mr. Greenstreet will keep you entertained till then."

The ten minutes passed, but the punctual Mr. Hardacre was not so punctual tonight. First five, then ten minutes late. We waited.

"Mr. Greenstreet, will you accompany me to Stateroom G?" The voice was anxious but clearly that of Allan Culbertson and, when I turned toward him, I saw the face behind his neatly trimmed beard was flushed.

"What is the matter?" Horace inquired.

"It's Mr. Hardacre. He's . . . he's been shot."

"Damn!" Horace bolted from his chair while the rest of our party followed behind. By the time we reached the

texas stairs, Horace had disappeared behind the door to the staterooms.

"I don't think you should come up," Culbertson warned, but I paid him no mind and made my way to the cabin of Elcid Hardacre.

Reaching the stateroom door, I found Horace and Dr. Cotton standing over a man at his writing desk. His head was down, with his right hand near his face, and the left hanging limply at his side. The most curious thing about the man in the chair, besides his attitude, was the cap on his head. It was Union blue, a private's cap that appeared too small for Hardacre's head. It was tilted to one side as if placed there to taunt the dead man. Dr. Cotton removed it from his head and hung it on the back of the chair. It was clear: The owner of the *Mississippi Girl* was beyond the help of Dr. Cotton.

"Where is the captain?" Horace asked as Culbertson reached the stateroom door.

"I've been unable to locate him. He may be down on the steerage deck."

"He should be notified at once." Horace considered the situation for a moment. "But there is no need to alarm the other passengers. Where are Mr. DuBois and his wife?"

"They are coming up the stairs now."

"Have them wait in the empty room down the hall. Then have the pilot come down from the pilothouse. He may have seen who has come and gone from the upper deck."

Culbertson turned to go, then stopped, staring at the floor. He picked up a large iron nail, examining it carefully. Horace's eyes met Culbertson's. It was the very same type that Captain McQuaid had used earlier in the saloon to clean his pipe. He set the nail on the sideboard, then turned to leave the room.

Dr. Cotton shook his head. "A single bullet in the chest," he said. "Close range, by the looks of it." It wasn't until then that Horace realized I was in the room. "Sadie, you can wait in our stateroom," he said.

"I'm all right," I said. "Go ahead with your investigation. Do what you must do."

I surprised myself with my own feelings. I looked at the dead man, not with revulsion, not with pity, nor horror, nor any other emotion one might expect. Instead, I felt a sort of cool detachment; it was as if it were a play I was viewing, and at any moment the curtain would come down and I could applaud the man at his desk for playing the part so well. In death, the man's face seemed to hold an expression which combined all his strengths and failures. I could clearly see his pride, his tenacity, his hardness of character. But there was something else in that face, something I couldn't quite put my finger on, something pitiable that made me wonder if anyone would mourn his passing.

I suddenly became aware of great activity outside. If it were a play I was watching, then surely it would be a farce. The whole thing had an incongruous air. Here was a dead man, killed by a bullet through the chest, while outside the celebration was again taking place. Firecrackers and firearms made reports in quick succession. Now and then through the open porthole window, the early night's leaden sky would be lit up by the flash from some unseen firework's display. Each flash was followed by expressions of approval from the passengers on the decks below.

I shook my head, returning to the room and the problem at hand. I was here to help Horace. Maybe if I listened and observed the facts, I could do just that.

"Can you fix a time to the murder?" Horace asked. "It may be important."

Dr. Cotton gave him an inquisitive look.

"I am a Pinkerton man."

"You don't say," the doctor murmured. He held Horace with his gaze, then returned toward the body. "During the war, I patched up a few hundred men. Seen a couple hundred more die. It may sound vain, but I figure I can fix a time of death about as well as any man alive."

The old physician began a systematic survey of the corpse. First, he put his hand to the dead man's forehead, then the back of the neck, and finally the hands. He lifted the arm that rested on the table, pulling back the sleeve, all the while making grunts of acknowledgment. The dead man's face was of special interest. He lifted each eyelid, poked at the cheeks and even opened the man's mouth, checking his tongue. He halted momentarily, as if startled by some newly uncovered fact. There was a small blue bottle, like those used by apothecaries, on the desk. Near the bottle was a half-full glass of red wine and, next to that, what appeared to be a ledger book. Horace, apparently finding some need to be tidy, closed the ledger. He moved it nearer the wine glass.

Meanwhile, Dr. Cotton read the label on the bottle. He drew his face very near to the dead man's. Finally, removing the scalpel he had previously used on his cigar, he scraped at the dried blood which was splattered on the desk. "This man has been dead between two and a half and three hours." He pulled out his chain watch and checked the time. "Three and a half hours at the outside, but no more."

Horace had pulled out the small leather-covered note pad from his pocket, jotting a few notes as Dr. Cotton spoke. "You are quite certain? As I said, this could be significant."

"There are three ways to set a time of death," Cotton explained. "Four if there is blood. Alone, none of these is accurate to any great degree, but taken together, with an experienced eye, one can come up with a time of death not too far off the mark."

Dr. Cotton again placed his hand to the dead man's forehead. "The first is temperature." Horace likewise followed suit, touching the forehead like a student following a professor's lead.

"The human body has a temperature right about ninety-nine degrees. When death occurs, that temperature slowly goes down until it matches the temperature of the air. The temperature of the air was eighty-four just a half hour ago. I checked it myself by the thermometer in my room. I'd estimate Hardacre's temperature is about half-way between ninety-nine and eighty-four. My best guess, from that fact alone, would set the time of death between two and six hours. Now, look at the lividity here."

"Lividity?"

"See here." Dr. Cotton lifted Hardacre's head to an upright position. "See where the skin is pale where it rested on the desk?"

Horace nodded.

"But the areas to the side where there was no pressure are beginning to discolor. These mottled, patchy areas of purple are where blood has settled after death. These areas are apparent around the eyelids and neck and indicate the first stages of what we call lividity."

"And what does that tell you about the time of death?" Horace asked.

"The first signs of lividity will usually occur in one to two hours. In this case, things are a trifle further along— say two to three hours."

Horace rolled a cigarette as he listened, and I realized how close the room now felt. I was getting a bit light-headed, and maybe not so composed as I first let on. I felt much the same as the time I was eight years old, and Billy Archer dissected a frog, carefully pulling out and naming her organs. I had forced myself to watch calmly, not giving him the pleasure of knowing it made me ill. I pinched myself hard in the arm just as I had some thirty-odd years past, then made my way to the open window. I wouldn't allow myself to faint or get sick now, either.

There was no wind to speak of, but it did feel cooler by the window. High in the sky, a silver-grey quarter moon, its horns pointing to the east, held command over an evening sky, with stars just becoming visible in the twilight. I saw silhouettes of men on the Cairo shore. Further on, the street lights were being lit one by one. The festivities outside continued. I looked again on the dead man's body. It occurred to me that I had truly left my old life, that comfortable, easy-chair life of some two days past and some six hundred miles to the north. I took a deep breath and rallied my nerve, then listened as Dr. Cotton resumed.

"Then there is the problem of the stiffness a body takes on after death."

"Rigor mortis."

"Exactly. This can vary greatly depending on how a

person dies. Why, I've seen one case in which a man's company was attacked as they sat around a campfire. The man was holding a coffee cup . . . " Dr. Cotton hesitated as his eyes met mine. "Let's just say it can take place straight away. More likely, it starts up in about three hours and is full-blown at six. This is more like your typical case; there are just now the beginnings of stiffness about the face and neck."

The doctor carefully wiped off his surgeon's knife on a handkerchief. "And the blood has had sufficient time to dry," he said, returning the scalpel to his breast pocket. "Yes, I'd say right about three hours. I'd stake my reputation on it."

"And that time would just about coincide with the celebration that took place," Horace murmured. "Is there anything else you can tell me?" asked Horace.

"There is one thing. It's a damnable odd thing too." Dr. Cotton pointed to the blue bottle that had caught his eye earlier.

But his explanation would have to wait. A knock on the door was followed by the figure of a very young man. He held a blue cap in his hand. It was the same cub pilot who had, only this morning, gallantly searched the river for the man who had gone overboard.

X

First Clues

———◆–▸◆◂–◆———

The young man stood at the threshold for a long moment, trying, it seemed, to elicit meaning from the scene before him. He ran a hand through his tousled hair, then, stepping forward, spoke with the clear voice of youth. "My name is Cooper. Thomas Cooper. I am the pilot's apprentice. I was told to come down here."

"Yes, Mr. Cooper. I am Horace Greenstreet. Please have a seat." Horace motioned to one of the corner chairs.

"What's going on here? Is he dead?"

"I'm afraid he is. Perhaps, with your help, we can get to the bottom of this."

Thomas Cooper pulled the red kerchief from around his neck and wiped his forehead. "How can I help?"

"Mr. Hardacre has been murdered. There is no question of that. According to Dr. Cotton, he was shot some three hours ago. Were you on duty at that time?"

"Yes, sir. I work the six-to-ten shift. On four, then off four, that's the way with pilots. Mr. Bixby—that's Mr. Josiah Bixby—is the master pilot on my shift."

"And where is he?"

"Down below, in his hammock, I reckon." The young man looked about nervously. "This is my first time alone in the pilothouse. Even though we're tied up and all, I shouldn't like Mr. Bixby to find out I left my post."

Horace made several notations on his note pad. "This will only take a few minutes, and then you can be about your business. What time was it when Mr. Bixby left you in charge?"

"It was half past six, just after our swing on the Mississippi. After we tied up again on the Cairo wharf, he said he'd be going below to speak to the captain."

"From the pilothouse you can see whoever comes or goes from the upper deck? Is that not correct?"

"Yes, sir, Mr. Greenstreet."

"Did you notice anyone coming or going from the time you came on duty until now?"

"Captain McQuaid made a couple of trips up and down the stairs; he left his room at six o'clock, then he returned and left again at six thirty."

"You are quite certain of these times?"

"Yes, sir. He was the one who told us to make a swing out to the Mississippi and back. At about six-twenty, he returned to his room, stayed for five or ten minutes, then left again. I know that time because we had just returned to the Cairo wharf, and Mr. Bixby left the pilothouse to talk to the captain and help with his trunk. That's when . . ."

"What the thunder was the captain doing with his trunk?"

"He was leaving the boat, sir."

Horace strode to the sideboard and picked up the nail which Culbertson had found on the floor. It was about three inches long with a broad, square head. He dropped the nail into his pants pocket. "I see," he said.

A gust of wind blew in from the window. That, along with the turning of conversation away from Mr. Hardacre's body, had made me feel more myself. I turned my attention to the young man. He wore his pilot's blue with obvious pride—all sharp cuffs and shiny brass buttons. Sitting in the large mahogany chair, he looked out of place, almost vulnerable. Sixteen, I thought to myself. Just about the age . . . I shook myself from my reverie just then. I wasn't about to dwell on the past today.

"Who else did you see coming or going from the upper rooms?" asked Horace.

"Dr. Cotton came and went a time or two, but I can't recall at what time," he said without looking the doctor's way. "And Mr. Culbertson came up right about just before nine." He thought for a moment. "For that matter, Mr. Hardacre himself came out of his cabin just after six. He came right up to the pilothouse and asked who had ordered us to leave Cairo wharf. When we told him it was the captain, Mr. Hardacre said we wouldn't have to worry about orders from an insolent captain for much longer."

Horace stepped up to the young man, extending his hand. "Thank you, Mr. Cooper. I commend you and your observant eye. We may wish further word with you later, but, for now, you may return to your duties."

Dr. Cotton waited for the door to close, then sprang to his feet more agilely than I had imagined possible. "This is not the work of Captain McQuaid," he said, pointing to

Hardacre's body. "I don't know why he left the boat, but I am sure there is an explanation. As for the nail in your pocket, it is clearly Captain McQuaid's, but it could have been dropped there anytime. Why, I've seen the nails he uses to clean his pipe lying about in every corner of this riverboat. Just because you find one . . ."

"That may be," Horace interrupted, raising an open hand. "But we will still have to ask why he left so suddenly." Horace returned to the desk. "I believe you were about to say something concerning this druggist's bottle."

Just as Horace had pulled the stopper, Dr. Cotton intervened. "Hell's bells, man! Don't be sniffing about with that bottle. There's a deadly poison in there."

Horace handed the bottle to Dr. Cotton. "Poison?"

"That's what I mean when I say it's a damnable odd thing. This bottle contains prussic acid. Have you heard of it?"

"It's a cyanide derivative, if I'm not mistaken," Horace said.

"Precisely," he said slowly, obviously impressed with Horace's knowledge. "But the handwriting on the bottle is what bothers me, Mr. Greenstreet." Dr. Cotton pointed to the label that read, "Pruss. Acid." "This is my handwriting—and my bottle of prussic acid. Why it is here on Mr. Hardacre's desk is beyond me."

"Are you saying that he was poisoned before he was shot?"

"Not at all," the physician explained. "A man shot after he's already dead doesn't bleed to any great extent. Mr.

Hardacre's death is definitely due to the wound in his chest."

Both men remained in puzzled silence for a time, a silence made more pronounced when I noticed that outside, the noises of celebration had momentarily ceased. Only the muffled notes of a piano resonated from the deck below.

"Is it possible he killed himself?" I said at last. "He may have been uncertain whether to use poison or a pistol, but in the end chose the pistol."

Horace gave my words some consideration, then began searching about the desk, in its drawers, at last removing a small bulldog revolver from Hardacre's jacket pocket. "Well, well," he said. "The more we study this affair, the more cloudy it becomes. There is a flap on the man's pocket, so the weapon could not have just fallen in." Horace smelled the muzzle, then turned toward me. "Why would a man place his gun in a pocket after shooting himself?"

Dr. Cotton waved his hand dismissively. "The man was shot at close range but not close enough for self-murder; I'd estimate the shot came from five to ten feet away."

Horace's hand moved in the direction of the ledger resting on Hardacre's desk. He drummed his fingers on it, a gesture I had seen before. He was perplexed about something. Possibly something in that ledger book, I thought as the drumming continued.

"Now, Dr. Cotton, I believe we have been given the

times of everyone coming or going from the upper deck with exception of you." Horace readied his note pad.

The doctor took his time before answering. As always, I listened as much with my eyes as with my ears. He twirled a cigar absentmindedly in his left hand like a small-town marshal twirls his baton. Presently, the cigar found its way between his teeth. He scratched a match and drew in. Without bothering to exhale, he began to speak. "There is a young lady in stateroom F." He pointed the cigar toward the room across the hallway.

"The one with the rinse in her hair," I said to myself.

Cotton continued, "She came to my cabin complaining of what we call *mal de mer,* that is to say, seasickness. It's not an uncommon thing, even on a riverboat tied to the dock. I made up a preparation of morphine and potassium bromide elixir to help her sleep. An elixir takes only a very short time to act. We talked for some ten minutes in my room until the elixir began to take effect, then I walked her back to her room."

Dr. Cotton took another puff from his cheroot. "As I returned to my room, I felt the boat beginning to move. Mr. Hardacre came flying out of his room just then. 'What the devil are those fools doing up in the pilothouse?' he says, pointing at me like I've got something to do with it. Well, Captain McQuaid had told me to be in the saloon about six, so I figured it was he that gave the orders, though I didn't let on. I just locked my door and made my way to the saloon. Hardacre was up in the wheelhouse by then, but he must have cooled down. I saw him returning to his room by the time I reached the middle deck."

"How long did you stay in the saloon?" Horace asked.

"It must have been nearly nine when I left. I hadn't been back in my room a minute before Mr. Culbertson was pounding at my door, telling me Hardacre'd been shot."

Horace drummed his fingers again on the ledger book. "If, as you say, you locked your cabin door, how is it that a bottle of poison from your room found its way to this desk?"

Dr. Cotton scratched his head but offered no answer. Slowly, his eyes raised and met those of Horace. "You don't think I had something to do with this?"

"Not at all," Horace reassured. "But you must admit it is a curious thing." Horace took the physician's elbow and began ushering him toward the door. "Your help has been invaluable, doctor. When the authorities arrive, I'm sure we will call on you again. Until then, I hope you will follow the advice I gave Mr. Culbertson and keep this affair to yourself."

He was taken aback by the swiftness which Horace had orchestrated his departure. Hesitating, he flashed me a perplexed look.

Horace is usually painstakingly precise, yet on occasion, he has flashes of abruptness. It is something I have grown accustomed to, but others find bordering on rudeness. "Perhaps you could see if anything besides the poison has been taken from your room," I said, trying to think of someway he might feel helpful. "I will keep you posted on any developments."

The smoke from his long cigar curled around his face as he squinted in my direction.

"One more thing," Horace said. "About the lady who you gave a sleeping potion."

"Yes."

"Did she tell you her name?"

"She didn't say what her full name was, but her family name is Atchison. Like I said before, I barely got her to her room after I gave her that sleeping draught. She'll be dead to the world until morning." Dr. Cotton looked back on the body of Hardacre and left the room.

"Atchison," Horace murmured, closing the door of Stateroom G.

XI

THE SCARLET LETTER

H orace shook the door handle, making sure it was locked. He walked to my side, placing a hand on my shoulder. "Are you sure you're all right?"

There was a full-length mirror on the wall next to me. Frowning, I regarded my reflection. I took a brief inventory: face slightly pale, the fine crow's feet on each side of my eyes a bit more noticeable than usual, brown eyes tired. Too many years looked back at me. "Do I look that bad?" I said, adjusting my silver hat pin.

"Not at all," Horace reassured. "I only meant this is more than either of us bargained for."

"He should have listened to you, Horace." I said. "Why is it so difficult for men to accept advice?" I didn't really expect an answer, but waited a moment just in case; then I asked, "What do you intend to do now?"

"The authorities in Cairo will have to be notified," he said. "A Pinkerton should never high-hat the locals. You never know if they will want your help or not. But I would like an hour's advantage before they arrive."

I gave him a quizzical look. "Advantage? You make it sound like a contest to find the murderer. Besides, the case appears perfectly clear to me. Captain McQuaid was here. His pipe nail shows that. He probably planned that business in the saloon to cause a distraction. Then, with the guns and fireworks going off, he came to Hardacre's room and shot him without anyone giving a notice to one more gunshot. He packs up and leaves and is heaven knows where. Meanwhile, we sit and talk of the stiffness a dead body takes on."

I could see Horace was not so certain of the captain's guilt. His expression took on that slightly self-satisfied look it always takes on when he knows something I do not. He walked back to Hardacre's desk.

"Quite an enlightening lecture the doctor gave, wouldn't you say, Sadie?"

"I thought it was most gruesome to be poking about a dead man's body."

"That may be, but I was particularly interested in his explanation of what he called lividity."

"Why so?"

"It is an interesting phenomenon, because I found the man's desk exhibits the very same property."

I fixed Horace with an impatient glance. "What the devil are you talking about?"

"Look here, Sadie." He pushed the ledger from its place on the desk. There was a stain in the wood, a dark red stain about two inches in height. It was in the shape of the letter 'A'.

I watched as Horace dipped a finger into the glass of wine. He made a mark on the table and compared it to the stain, first with his eyes then with fingers.

"You think it is a message left by Hardacre?" I asked.

"It is possible. You notice there are no other markings on the surface. Mr. Hardacre doesn't seem the type to make idle markings on his desk."

"What a strange way to leave a message," I said. "Why didn't he just use a pen?"

"Yes, that is odd." There was a steel-nib pen in a holder not far from the glass of wine, and Horace inspected it. Satisfied that it was in working order, Horace spoke, and his words seemed aimed more to himself than to me. "The only thing we can say with certainty is that Mr. Hardacre knew the person who killed him. I did warn against opening his door to anyone, but, as you say, he wasn't in the habit of taking advice. Even so I don't believe he would be so reckless as to let in just anybody."

He removed the pipe nail from his pocket. "On the other hand, there may be a pattern here. A pattern of false messages. A soldier's cap, Captain McQuaid's nail, a bottle of poison belonging to Dr. Cotton, and the letter 'A', which could stand for Allan Culbertson. If Dr. Cotton is correct, it could even refer to the young lady named Atchison who recently came aboard. Four possible suspects already, and we have not yet searched the room thoroughly. It seems to me someone is attempting to confound the issue."

Horace brushed at his side whiskers with the back of his hand. "Remember, the captain carried his trunk with him, a fairly large trunk from the sound of it. It is unlikely a man attempting to escape justice would do so." He looked at me in a contemplative manner. "There is no doubt a union hall in Cairo, and I expect that would be the first place an out-of-work captain would go. Someone must go into town to alert the authorities and to find out what has become of Captain McQuaid." He paused. "I'm not sure who we can trust here, Sadie."

Horace knew me all too well. He knew just how to push my pride. He knew that, without consideration of the hour or the fact that I would rather have stayed and helped with the investigation, I would volunteer.

"I will go," I said at last. "The night air will do me good."

There must have been air currents in the room, for the oil lantern flickered and sputtered, casting shafts of yellow light on Horace's face. He reached inside his leather boot, producing a small-caliber pistol. It was a single-shot derringer; it was the very gun he had bought for me in California so many years past, the one I had not yet fired.

"A Pinkerton shouldn't be without a gun," he said, placing the smoky-pearl handle in my palm. "This case has taken several untoward turns, and I am not certain we have seen the last of the unexpected. I do not wish you to be unprepared." Horace regarded the scarlet letter, then said, "What did you make of the young pilot's apprentice, Sadie? Can he be trusted?"

"He seemed a likable boy. Why do you ask?"

"You will need someone to accompany you. If I am not mistaken, you will find a U.S. Marshal in Cairo by the name of John Thurmond. He is the man to see. Tell him everything, then inquire about Captain McQuaid at the Union Hall. If he cannot be found or is unwilling to return, then we will let Mr. Thurmond take care of that matter."

"What are you going to do?" I asked.

"I plan to interview everyone else who has had access to these staterooms. It is always the best policy to question those involved immediately, before they can solidify false stories in their minds."

I was just about to ask Horace whom he suspected when the knocker again sounded on the stateroom door. I discreetly slipped the derringer into my handbag and slipped the ledger over the scarlet letter as Horace opened the door.

"Ah! Mr. Culbertson. You have come to inform us that you were unable to find Captain McQuaid on board."

"Yes. I also spoke with Dr. Cotton in the hall. He tells me you are a Pinkerton."

"I was hired by Hardacre after he received a death threat." Horace gave the man a long, hard look. "I thought you knew."

"No," Culbertson replied quickly. "I was not privy to all of Mr. Hardacre's business."

"But you are the purser. You must know a great deal about the workings of the riverboat. Especially those of a financial nature."

Culbertson pulled at his beard and, as he did so, I noticed a reddish smear on his white shirt cuff. "I guess I do," he replied.

It appeared as if the observation was not shared by Horace, for he resumed his questioning of the purser. "Was Mr. Hardacre in the habit of keeping money in his room?"

Culbertson motioned toward the wall and the portrait of Hardacre's father. "There is a combination safe behind that picture. He keeps the table winnings and other profits from the saloon in there." Horace strode to the wall and stood below the portrait of Hardacre's father as Culbertson continued, "The safe was imported from Switzerland and is pick-proof. Hardacre once boasted that the wall would have to come down if ever he died since the code numbers were kept only in his head."

Horace brushed his hand across the bottom of the picture frame. After removing the elder Hardacre from a wall nail, he began turning the dial three times, beginning in a clockwise manner. Upon reaching the final position, he pulled up on the safe's lever. The lock remained fast.

"I told you the safe is impenetrable," the purser said, amused. He gave me a condescending shake of the head.

Horace, however, remained unperturbed and began the process all over again. He reached the final digit, then reached for the handle. The door of the safe swung open.

"That safe is . . ." Mr. Culbertson never finished his sentence, so at a loss was he for words. Horace looked at us blandly. The oil lantern flickered. I rubbed my cat's-eye pendant.

Horace peered into the open space momentarily, then swung the metal door closed. "As much as I would like to inspect the contents of Mr. Hardacre's safe, I think it best we wait for the marshal.

"Now, Mr. Culbertson," he resumed, pointing to the adjoining room. "I understand Mr. Hardacre kept that room empty for unexpected guests."

"You might say that."

"Would you be so kind as to use your key and open it?"

"What makes you think I have a key?" Culbertson returned, with a voice now somewhat defensive.

"You are the purser, are you not?"

Culbertson shrugged. "It so happens I do have a key. What do you want in that room?"

"We will need a place to question everyone who might be involved in this business." Horace glanced at the body. "I don't think this room will be suitable."

The purser pulled out a key chain and moments later swung the door open. I could see only a small portion of the adjoining compartment, which was dominated by a dark wood four-poster with a creme-colored canopy.

"I have just a few remaining questions," Horace said as he made a notation in his memorandum book. "The key in your hand must be a master key for all the staterooms. Who else possesses such a key?"

The purser's look was guarded, but he answered with only a slight hint of hesitation. "Mr. Hardacre had one, along with Captain McQuaid."

"I see. The other question concerns Mr. Hardacre's body. When you found him at his desk, did you touch the body?"

"No. I went directly to Dr. Cotton's room. I was certain the man was dead, but I thought the doctor should be the one to examine him."

Horace took the man's arm, turning it slightly. "Then how do you explain the fact you have blood on your sleeve?"

A flash of anger passed over Culbertson's face for an instant. Then he put a hand to his face and thought for a moment. "I cannot say for sure how I came by it. One is driven by instincts in cases like this. Possibly I did touch the body to make sure he was dead. I must have done so, but I do not recall it."

"Yes," Horace mused. "I quite understand. When one is in an urgent situation, it is difficult to recall exactly how events transpired." Horace looked at his note pad. "This new passenger, the young lady who has a stateroom just across the hall—do you know her name?"

"No, but I could check the register."

"That won't be necessary just now. Dr. Cotton has given her a sleeping draught, and we will not be able to question her till morning. Is there a particular chambermaid who cleans Mr. Hardacre's room?"

"That would be Nellie Dawes."

Horace made a note of the name.

"Thank you, Mr. Culbertson," bringing the interview to an end. "Please inform Mr. DuBois and his wife that I will be in to see them momentarily. They will be required to stay aboard at least until the marshal arrives."

XII

YOUNG
MASTER COOPER

———◆◆◆———

H ardacre was correct," Horace said when the purser had gone. "Mr. Culbertson is certainly quick on his feet. He explained away that blood stain without so much as the bat of an eye. What do you think, Sadie?"

"I think that by Dr. Cotton's reckoning of the time Hardacre was shot, Culbertson couldn't be the murderer. He was with us in the saloon. It still seems to me that Captain McQuaid is the most logical suspect."

"Then I suggest you leave at once for the city."

"You know you can't get off quite that easily, husband."

I looked again to the mirror and made a few minor adjustments with the aid of a hair brush and tin of rice powder. Horace lit a candle and was assessing the adjoining room. When he returned, he found me waiting in the doorway, hand on hip.

"All right, all right, Sadie," he said. "I'll tell you. But, I really shouldn't. You'll only be disappointed. You wouldn't ask a magician to tell you his secrets."

"I would if the magician were my husband."

He took my hand and led me to where the portrait of
the senior Hardacre was secured over the safe. The man's
eyes were hard like his son's, and, as I read aloud the name
written below the picture, I thought how fitting that name
was. Below the name were the dates of his birth and death.
They were written, curiously, in the common shorthand,
each with three groups of two numbers, signifying a
month, day, and year. I reflected for a moment on Poe's
"The Purloined Letter." The answer was so simple, one
could not fail to overlook it. "Have you read the detective
stories of Poe?" I asked.

"No," he said, and looked surprised.

I kissed Horace's cheek. "I will be back in an hour or
two. Did you say the marshal's name is Thurmond?"

"Yes. John Thurmond," he said distractedly.

I left him there in stateroom G, and, although I didn't
tell him, I was not disappointed.

Outside, the night air remained warm, filled with an
earthy smell, not unpleasant, and occasionally com-
pounded with the scent of burning hickory from some unseen kitchen stove. The westward sky was dark, covered
by a series of rifted clouds that retained just a hint of sun-
set orange. Overhead the sky was darker still, except for a
silvery moon. Somewhere in the distance, the low thud of
a woodman's ax seemed to keep perfect time with a low
throbbing in my head. There were laudanum drops in my
bag, and I considered taking out the bottle, but then remembered how drowsy they always made me. And tonight
might be a very long night. I took a deep breath and looked
up toward the pilothouse. There were two shadows in the

windows, and, although I could make out neither, I recognized the voice of one to be Thomas Cooper. The other was, in all probability, a second apprentice.

The two spoke loosely, with the bravado of male adolescence, peppering their speech now and again with a well-placed cuss, the kind which always seems out of place coming from the lips of youth. I eavesdropped for a moment despite myself and could occasionally make out bits

and phrases. The names Hardacre and Pinkerton were spoken more than once. When they saw I was making my way up the staircase, the windowed cubicle became quiet. The older of the two took off his leather-billed cap and held it crumpled in his left hand when I opened the door. Unlike his counterpart, Thomas Cooper was out of the pilot-blue jacket and was now wearing a civilian shirt and trousers with brown leather braces.

"Excuse me, Master Cooper. Am I interrupting important business?"

"No, ma'am. My shift is over, and I was just getting ready to go below."

"Are you familiar with the streets of Cairo?" I asked.

The young man looked to his companion before returning a shrug. "I guess so," he said. "The main street, leastways."

"You were very helpful down below, and I was wondering if you could be so again."

"You want me to go for the police?" he asked.

"Actually, I was hoping you would accompany me," I said.

The young man looked a bit disappointed, but after some further discussion agreed, and as we made our way down three staircases and off the *Mississippi Girl,* I explained our mission.

He walked with a spring to his step, which I found was both contagious and difficult to match. We crossed the levee and looked up Commercial Avenue. Like those of most towns that had grown piecemeal, the streets of Cairo were narrow and set at odd angles to the main commercial street, which was wide, well-lit with lanterns, and flanked by boardwalks on either side. Its cobblestone was chipped and rusty with ruts caused by wheeled traffic.

Thomas Cooper pointed to a white-washed building set back a few feet from the boardwalk. "There's the union hall," he said. A light was shining from a window. The door was unlocked. Entering, we looked upon a rather cheerless room with high rafters where a haze of old blue smoke and a maze of grey cobwebs hung. A low, flat-topped stove, around which were positioned five wooden chairs, centered the room. A deck of cards and two empty glasses on the stove indicated it had taken on new duties since last winter. The wall to my left was nearly covered by a map depicting the Mississippi, Ohio, and Missouri river system. Six pine benches faced the map, situated like pews in a church. To the right was a moth-tattered pool table. My inspection of the room was cut short by the voice and figure of an elderly man entering the rear doorway. He stood for a moment on the threshold with a questioning look on his face and small crate in his hands. "This is a union hall, ma'am. Tea house is in the St. Charles two doors down."

"I am not looking for a tea house; I am looking for . . . I'm looking for my husband."

"And who might that be?" he said, placing the crate on the pool table.

"My husband was formerly captain of the riverboat *Mississippi Girl*. My name is Mrs. McQuaid, and this is our son. We were told to meet him in Cairo but I'm afraid I've forgotten which hotel."

"I don't believe he ever mentioned a wife." The old man lifted an officer's cap and scratched his head. "Well, it's too late. He left about an hour ago. Didn't say where he was staying tonight, but he'll be back first thing in the morning. He just took a berth with the *Northern Star* out of St. Paul. She's scheduled for departure at nine o'clock sharp."

"Are you certain he'll be back?"

"He's got to sign his orders. Those are the rules. He'll be back tomorrow."

"Please tell him we urgently need to see him and will be waiting for him in Stateroom E on the *Mississippi Girl.*"

Thomas Cooper was a fast study. He took my arm. "Come along, mother," he said. The words produced in me an eerie feeling. He gave me an admiring smile as we stepped out into the street. "You do that well," he said.

"Sometimes deceit is necessary," I said. "We don't want the whole town to know what has happened. At least not yet. It sounds as if Captain McQuaid is unaware of the murder. If that is so, he may be more inclined to return to the *Mississippi Girl* out of curiosity than if he knew he was suspected of a crime."

"What if he has committed the murder?" Thomas Cooper asked.

I shrugged. "At least he will know that someone is looking for him. He will either run, or may feel it is wisest to return and hope that a case cannot be made against him."

We walked arm-in-arm for a while, each a bit self-conscious, I suppose. He was probably attempting to cling to that adolescent bravado, while I was beginning to feel an uneasiness because I knew why I had taken an interest in the young man.

A few shops were lighted on the street, taking advantage of those holiday revelers who had not found their way home. We passed a millinery, and I was distressed to find the window mannequin staring at me was wearing my hat. The young man must have noticed it too. He cocked his head. "It looks better on you," he said, and I smiled.

From an open upstairs window, the smell of someone's dinner made me hungry. I reached into my oversized reticule. "Chocolate?" I asked. Further on I said, "It must be quite a responsibility. Piloting a riverboat, I mean."

"Not really." He unwrapped a second chocolate. "I guess it was in the old days, before the river was dredged. Then a pilot had to know every snag, every shoal, then re-learn it again each time the water level changed. Now it's like riding a horse down Main Street. We just follow the markers. My uncle was a pilot in those days, and he helped me get my appointment. But I can see there's no future to it."

"Really? Why is that?"

"The railroads have taken over most of the river business. There's two out-of-work pilots for every one with a billet."

"What will you do?" I asked.

"Maybe I'll go to California. I'd like to see San Francisco."

"Where are your parents?"

"They died when I was young. I was raised by my uncle . . . the one who was the riverboat pilot."

"I'm sorry."

He shrugged. "I never really knew them, so I don't think about it much."

"How old are you now?"

"Sixteen."

"Ironic," I said in a whisper and forced a smile. I was silent for a long while as my mind continued on. My own son would have been just sixteen. He died of consumption while we were in California. It was just after that when I slowly retreated to my books, my writing, and my easy chair. It was a full city block later before I realized I had been lost in my thoughts.

"Are you all right?"

"Yes, you'll have to excuse me. I have a tendency to think too much."

He turned down a third chocolate. "I never heard of a lady Pinkerton."

"Actually, my husband is the Pinkerton. I am just helping him." He looked disappointed, so I said, "There are few women in the Agency. But, maybe, just maybe . . ."

We had walked seven or eight blocks up the main street and were now approaching a city square, where a great pile of cannonballs were stacked neatly in a pyramid. An American flag flapped in the breeze as a man worked a pulley to bring it down for the night. Thomas Cooper asked for directions, and the man pointed to a brown stone building.

"The marshal's office is first door on the left."

The wind blew briskly from the Mississippi side of town, bringing with it those clouds I had observed earlier in the westward sky. A scruffy street gamin, dressed in patched trousers, was hawking newspapers in front of the building. He had one paper left and, seeing the banner of the *Chicago Tribune,* I asked, "Yesterday's or today's?"

"Today's," he answered. "Just off the train an hour ago. It's my last one."

I handed him a nickel for the four-cent paper. "I don't have any change," he lied. He stuffed the coin in his shirt pocket, and I stuffed the folded paper into my reticule.

We entered the courthouse. The first door on the left had a large pane of glass and was held open by a triangular block of wood. A name was painted on the opposite side of the glass, and I read it backwards: JOHN QUINCY THUR-MOND, U.S. MARSHAL. Set in the crack between glass and frame was a faded playing card, a jack of spades. Curious. From inside came the off-key whistling of an undistinguishable song. I knocked, and we entered.

I was unnerved to find a man leaning back in a chair, casually rolling a cigarette in that same one-handed manner Horace employed. And that wasn't all that made me uneasy. There were his eyes. To be more precise, his left eye. He had a loose eyeball—glass, I suppose—that didn't go where the other one went, but rolled crazily in the socket as if with a mind of its own. It was an irritant, that eyeball, for I soon found I could hardly talk to the man without watching the eye go this way and that and wondering where it would end up. Etched into his sunburnt face was the vague outline of an eye-patch. I wished he would have left it on.

"I am looking for Marshal Thurmond," I said.

The man in the chair raised his eye. "You found him."

"My name is Sadie Greenstreet, and this is Thomas Cooper. We have come to report a murder aboard the *Mississippi Girl.*"

He listened to my story in a distracted sort of way at first, like a man with plenty of time and no particular place to go. But his posture improved steadily as I reconstructed the facts of the case. When I had concluded, the marshal dampened his lantern without a word, and, as the light faded, I watched him tuck an ominous-looking pistol into his belt. He ushered us out of the office. "You say your husband is a Pinkerton man?" he said. It might have been my imagination, but I could swear I saw a smile cross his face.

"Yes. Horace Greenstreet is his name. He works out of Chicago."

As he locked the door behind him, I could just make out the back side of the playing card. It appeared Marshal John Quincy Thurmond was lacking for an eye but not for a sense of humor.

XIII

ONE-EYED JACK
AND THE CHAMBERMAID

———♦·◆·♦———

The streets of Cairo had thinned out. Insects
swarmed around street lanterns, but it seemed
nearly all human activity had now retreated behind the two
saloon doors located at opposite ends of the main street.

Thomas Cooper gave Marshal Thurmond the particulars of the affair from his pilothouse perspective, while I
reflected on the details from my own.

According to Horace, when faced with a problem,
sometimes it is best to restate the dilemma. Only when the
large picture is perfectly clear should the smaller details be
added. Most often it is a small detail that acts like glue to
piece those larger facts together.

Now it seemed to me there were three main incidents,
separate but related. First, Hardacre receives the threatening notes. Originally, we thought the letters might have
been hoaxes written by Hardacre himself, but this seemed
less likely now. The fact that the letters were delivered by
a local carrier and not through the mail indicated the
sender was nearby. This would mean he would have to
have been in Cincinnati when we departed. Dr. Cotton,

Captain McQuaid, or Culbertson would be the prime suspects. Mr. DuBois could be a possibility only if he had an accomplice.

I listened for a moment as Marshal Thurmond asked the cub pilot a few questions about Hardacre. We were three blocks from the levee, and I could see the night lights on the *Mississippi Girl* shining as if nothing were amiss. A Negro teamster with a load of milled lumber passed us by, his body bent over the reins like a question mark. I let my mind drift back to my thoughts.

The second related incident was the burglary in our stateroom. Only the threatening letter, along with a few of Horace's Pinkerton papers, was stolen. Whoever was responsible was either a passenger or a crew member. Culbertson, Captain McQuaid, and Hardacre himself had keys to all the staterooms. Of course, others could have stolen a key or had a new one made—Dr. Cotton or even the chambermaid. What was her name? Oh, yes, Nellie Dawes.

Finally, we come to the murder of Hardacre. At this point things get less clear, since we have to depend on Dr. Cotton's estimate for the time of death. The three people who boarded at Cairo must also be considered. The woman whose name is Atchison was in her stateroom at the time of the murder. But Dr. Cotton states she was given a sleeping potion. He also says Hardacre went up to the pilothouse after the doctor had walked her to her room.

Mr. and Mrs. DuBois were with us in the saloon, so they are even less likely candidates. Besides, none of the newcomers could have written the note in Cincinnati, or broken into our stateroom.

That again leaves Culbertson, Dr. Cotton, and Captain McQuaid. Culbertson was with us in the saloon, so he can be eliminated. The same is true for Dr. Cotton; that leaves Captain McQuaid. Again, all this presumes Dr. Cotton is correct, and has not lied, about the time of death. And what about the almost-too-obvious clues—a pipe nail, a bottle of poison, and the letter 'A'—not to mention the Union cap. Very confusing.

I could see I was getting nowhere, and was glad to find we had reached the levee and the *Mississippi Girl*. At least the problem was clear in my mind. Now if I could just find the glue to piece it together.

We boarded the riverboat at last, and, after climbing the twenty-eight stairs to the texas deck, the marshal dismissed Thomas Cooper. In the dim light, I noticed that same odd smile appear on the lawman's face. Almost at once I felt ill-at-ease, though I couldn't say exactly why.

"Third door on the right," I said when he gave me a questioning glance.

We entered stateroom E, the room adjacent to Hardacre's. Horace was in an apricot-colored winged chair. His note pad was in one hand and an unlit cigarette in the other. Looking up, he had a disoriented expression on his face as if his mind couldn't register what he was seeing. In a moment, I discovered why.

Marshal Thurmond had taken a step forward. Then, slowly, almost mechanically, he unbuttoned his jacket, pulled out the eight-inch horse pistol and, pointing it straight at Horace, said, "Well, well, Horace Greenstreet, here we are. I've waited five years for this. Five years. And now I'm going to collect . . . with interest. You do remember, Horace, don't you?"

I was in a state of shock. For a brief moment, I felt faint. The next, I was charged with electricity, the kind of feeling you get when you're dozing off and suddenly you realize your carriage is traveling on only two wheels.

I am often compulsive, but this time my mind ran through a list of possible solutions to this problem. In a Topeka bar I had seen a young man kick a gun from the hand of the town sheriff to save his friend from arrest. It had cost him a broken jaw and two years of hard labor. Besides being a woman, I was twenty years older than the young man, and the dress I was wearing would make a kick difficult at best.

I could run in front of Horace and tell the marshal he'd have to shoot me first. But Marshal Thurmond didn't appear the type swayed by pity.

Then it came to me. My derringer. I reached into my reticule and pushed away the first layer of chocolates. I dug deeper; damn chocolates! You may remember I mentioned having three vices. You now know the second. I dug deeper and found a confectioner's tin. Nearly in panic, I pushed past my rice-powder rouge, and my fingers slipped around a steel finger guard. I pulled it out, drawing a bead on the marshal's infernal glass eye. I took a step in his direction and, with a deep breath, jacked the lever and stood stock still before him. Still—except for the slight quavering of the derringer. "Hold it there, mister, or I'll shoot that glass eye from its socket."

He gave me a hard look with his good eye, turned back to Horace, then raised his hands and gun sheepishly. Horace leaped from his chair and strode forward. The two men stared at each other for several seconds, then broke into the most raucous laugh I ever heard.

In mild amusement, mild irritation, and, finally, not-so-mild-embarrassment, I watched the two carry on at my expense for several minutes.

Marshal Thurmond had a deep-timbre laugh, the kind that seems to fairly vibrate the walls and rafters. Horace's own laugh has always been quite infectious, reminiscent of a high-pitched Gatling gun. At one point, I had to bite my upper lip for fear I might be drawn in. By and by the laughter died, and as they turned their gazes back to me, I thought I could read a measure of admiration in both their faces.

Horace removed the derringer from my hand, carefully releasing the lever. Without knowing it, I had been pointing the little pistol at the marshal the entire time. I wondered if I could have actually used it. Probably not. But they didn't know that.

Horace reached in his pocket and thumbed a five-dollar gold piece into the air. "Square?" he asked. The coin dropped into the marshall's hand.

"Square," he said. "Does she know the story?"

Horace shook his head.

"Your husband played a little trick on me a few years back in Ellsworth," he said to me. "I'm surprised he never told you."

"It appears Horace doesn't tell me everything," I said, looking at my husband.

Thurmond seemed not to hear. "That was a time, eh, Horace?" He buttoned his twill-weave jacket. "Now, what's all this about a murder?"

Horace shook his head. "It's a queer business, but it looks to be the work of the ship's captain." He gave me an interrogative tilt of the head.

"I inquired at the union office as you suggested," I said. "He's taken a position with a commercial boat called the *Northern Star.* The boat is bound for St. Paul and is scheduled to leave Cairo at nine tomorrow morning."

Horace pointed to the open doorway. "The body's in there."

I contented myself to stay put as the two men passed through the communicating door and entered Hardacre's stateroom. I took a seat and listened as Horace briefed Marshal Thurmond about Dr. Cotton's findings, the possible suspects, where each was at the time of the murder, and, finally, the curious set of clues left in the room.

As they spoke, I let my eyes roam about Stateroom E. The room was the same dimensions as the others on the high deck, yet seemed considerably more spacious due to the lack of furniture. A mahogany bureau, a four-poster, the horsehair chair I was sitting on, and a small cherrywood wall clock were its only furnishings. A rather plump lady looked down at me from a picture above the bed, quite nude except for the lacy white hat on her head. I regarded the woman's headgear and her reclining ample figure for a few moments, then returned a half-eaten chocolate back into my handbag. Pamela would be a little nettled with me, sitting there, a room away from the men, a room away from those investigating a crime. But I felt comfortable sitting in the comfortable chair, which reminded me of my own.

Through the yellow-orange lantern light, the lawman and the detective traced about the room, their figures casting eerie shadows on the dark walls. Every now and then the deep voice of Thurmond would ask a question, which Horace answered in his slow, precise manner. The safe was again opened, apparently revealing a number of documents and a large amount of money. I heard Horace's voice say, "My wife can go through these papers in the morning, assuming we still need to after we question Captain McQuaid. Hardacre's will may be among them." Horace paused. "That is, if you think you might need a couple of extra hands."

Before Thurmond could answer, the knocker on Stateroom G was softly sounded. It was a timid knock and an equally timid voice I heard say, "I am Nellie Dawes, the chambermaid. You wish to see me?"

I quickly pulled the coverlet from the bed and raced into Hardacre's room. I draped it over the body before the maid was aware of what was happening, then stood in front of the body. "Perhaps you would be more comfortable in the next room?" I said, giving Horace a pointed look. It is quite amazing how even a man of Horace's intellect can, at times, be so thick when it comes to sensibilities. Horace ran his fingers through his hair and appeared ready to speak, but it was Marshal Thurmond who broke the awkward silence.

"Yes, Mrs. Greenstreet is correct. I believe we would be more comfortable in the adjoining room." Thurmond ushered the woman into stateroom E, where she took a seat in the only chair.

She was about sixty, a well-kept sixty with only faint traces of grey in her auburn hair. She seemed to possess a sort of nervous energy. Her hands were constantly in motion, smoothing her apron, adjusting an out-of-place hair, or merely wringing her hands as if they held a damp cleaning cloth. I could imagine those hands and that energy making quick work of her chores. Very green eyes looked about the room anxiously. They were clear eyes that made a striking contrast to her hair.

"I am Marshal John Thurmond. Are you aware of the situation?" Thurmond asked, looking back toward Hardacre's stateroom.

She paused, as if unsure of her answer. "I am," she said at last. "Dr. Cotton thought I should know. I often clean Mr. Hardacre's room early in the morning, and he didn't want me to be shocked by what I would find."

Horace stood near the window, making jottings on his note pad, while I looked on from the doorway.

"I see," said the marshall. He gave Horace an uneasy look, and I could see he had no idea why Horace had called for her. For that matter, neither did I. Thurmond cleared his throat. "Well, Horace, I guess this sort of questioning is more up your alley. Anything you want to ask her?"

"If you don't mind, I do have a question or two for Mrs. Dawes. It is Mrs., isn't it?"

She nodded her head. "It is, though I've been a widow for some fifteen years."

"How long have you worked for Hardacre?"

"I was housekeeper for the elder Mr. Hardacre in St. Louis since before the war. After he died, I stayed on till the time his son built the *Mississippi Girl* and sold the old estate. I stayed not out of loyalty, you understand, for I felt little loyalty to the new master, and wasn't paid but very stingily. But women of my age have few choices. When work was done on this riverboat, he asked me if I wouldn't take the job of chambermaid, and it's here I've been for the best part of six months."

More jottings, then Horace asked, "How do you get into the rooms to clean them?"

"With my key, of course." She pulled a brass key from her apron.

Horace raised his brows and glanced back at me. "Mr. Culbertson said there were only three keys to the stateroom, his own, Captain McQuaid's, and Hardacre's."

"Well, I guess Mr. Culbertson doesn't know everything," she said.

Presently, the wall clock rang its chime twelve times. As we waited for the final strike, Mrs. Dawes rose from her chair, wound the clock's spring, then returned to her chair with a rather sheepish expression. "You'll have to pardon me. Old habits, you know. I cleaned the room today— that is . . . yesterday," she said, looking back at the clock, "and I just remembered I had forgotten to wind the clock."

She looked down at her hands. They were still wringing out that imaginary cleaning rag.

"Your conscientiousness is admirable," Horace said. "I assume you cleaned Mr. Hardacre's room as well."

"Yes, I came by at three o'clock. Mr. Hardacre usually left at that time, but yesterday he stayed at his desk while I cleaned the room."

"I take it you did a thorough job?"

The chambermaid's face held an indignant expression.

"What I mean to say is, there is no chance that something, say a nail or some such, could have been left lying on the floor and not swept up?"

She answered him levelly and in a word, "No."

Horace removed himself from the room, returning moments later with the private's cap, nail, and poison bottle. "Have you ever seen these items before?"

The chambermaid looked at them carefully. "The medicine bottle is like those in Dr. Cotton's quarters, and the nail is like those used by Captain McQuaid to clean his pipe. He's always leaving them about. I think he does it on purpose so he always has one handy." She turned her gaze toward the cap. "But I'm sure I never saw this before."

"You are quite certain it wasn't Mr. Hardacre's cap?"

"Mr. Hardacre was never a soldier. Far from it. When you're as rich as Hardacre, you can hire a man to take your son's place. His father sent him off to England when the fighting began."

Horace pulled at his side-whiskers, "I see," he said reflectively, "Do you recall when Mr. Hardacre made the curious-looking wine stain on his desk?"

Nellie Dawes drew herself up as if ready to spring to her feet and take care of that spill. She checked herself. "It's true, Mr. Hardacre drank a good deal. Too much, if you ask me, especially for a man in his condition. But I never saw him spill a drop in all the time I've been with him. There was never a wine stain on his desk. At least there wasn't one when I left him in the afternoon."

Horace pulled the watch chain from his pocket, fingering it slowly without checking its time. It was his counterpart to my cat's-eye pendant, and I knew his interest was piqued. "You say, 'a man in his condition.' Exactly what condition do you mean?"

"I guess I can say now," she said, looking about the room in her high-strung way. "He didn't want anyone to know about it, but he was a sick man. A very sick man."

Lightning flashed somewhere in the distance, momentarily spreading its light around the stateroom. I looked down at my right ankle, where a dull pain was radiating up my leg. I was five when I broke that ankle. Ever since, it would always begin aching just before a change in the weather.

Besides the ache in my foot, I was beginning to feel tired and just a little detached. For about the third or fourth time since we left Chicago, I wondered if I really belonged here. Horace had asked another question or two, but I only heard the mumble of voices. A minute or more must have passed, then the chambermaid rose from her chair.

When she reached the door, I heard Horace say. "One more thing, Mrs. Dawes." He was rolling a cigarette now, still as fresh and confident as when he'd just had his haircut and shave. "What were you doing between the hours of six and seven o'clock?"

She answered quickly. Too quickly, it seemed, as if she'd prepared for the question. "I believe I was in my quarters on the steerage deck," she said.

Horace nodded. "Thank you, Mrs. Dawes." Nellie Dawes left the room.

Marshal Thurmond had been silent since he let Horace conduct the interview. Presently, he ran a hand across his face as if checking that day's growth. "She's an old lady, Horace. You made it sound like you suspected her."

Horace tilted his head and furrowed his brow as if to say, "I suspect everyone." The wind was picking up outside. I listened to the whistling noise it was making, and thought about the chambermaid.

THE
ANTIVIVISECTION
LEAGUE

I took in a deep breath, glad to be back in my own stateroom. It had been a long day, and I was just now feeling its effects. I could vaguely make out the smell of a
bonfire burning somewhere in the distance. If my ankle
was correct, that fire wouldn't be burning much longer.

Mr. and Mrs. DuBois were in stateroom D, and Horace had gone to speak to them. They would have to stay
aboard until the matter was cleared up, which with luck
would be in the morning. Marshal Thurmond said he
would go to the *Northern Star* and make certain the riverboat and Captain McQuaid wouldn't leave Cairo without
his consent. Horace and the marshal had agreed to a seven
o'clock meeting, when they would speak with the young
lady in stateroom F and await the arrival of Captain Mc-
Quaid.

I set my newspaper on the bed and reached for my
laudanum bottle. With all the thoughts running through
my head and a storm brewing outside, I knew that, despite

the hour, it would be difficult to fall asleep. But the drops always left my mind cloudy in the morning, and I returned the corked bottle to the side table. Horace had left a half-smoked cigarette in a receptacle, and I resolved to smoke it instead. I had smoked a few before and always found they calmed my nerves.

I undid my hair and ran a brush through it several times. The tired reflection that stared back at me from the mirror looked like a stranger. I set the looking-glass face down on the table. I was not accustomed to this new life, and there was enough in my mind without worrying about crow's feet and flecks of greying hair. I drew in deeply from the last of the cigarette.

Sitting on the edge of the quilt-covered bed, my eyes were drawn to an article in the second column of the newspaper, directly below a notice for homeopathic remedies. It must have been intuition, for I felt a sinking feeling in the pit of my stomach. I instinctively reached for my pendant. 'Four Women Arrested,' the headline said. I read on:

> Four women, all members of a group calling them-selves The Antivivisection League, were arrested last night near the home of Dr. Ronald Milton of Chesborough Lane. According to arresting officer Patrick Gilde, the four were picketing the Milton home because of his use of animals for scientific ex-perimentation. When the renowned doctor refused to speak to the assemblage, a certain Miss Pamela Paine, of 121 Lake Street, dispatched a brick through the doctor's front window.

"Damn!" I said under my breath, but I had to smile despite myself. Pamela always had good aim. I remembered our childhood and the three rocks she had sent through Widow McGilray's windows. The attack was called for in our minds when we found three poisoned cottontails in the old woman's garden. A window for each rabbit was our idea of juvenile justice. Things were simple back then. And, back then, Pamela had not been caught. I read on:

> Miss Paine, who acted as spokesman for these advocates of animals, stated that the group will not rest until Dr. Milton ceases his activities. The four were released on $100 bond and are due for arraignment before the magistrate next Tuesday.
>
> This latest incident underscores a recent increase in social activism among a small number of local women. It is this reporter's opinion that the average Chicagoan takes a dim view of the wholly unladylike manner in which these women rabble-rousers conduct themselves. Although we do not condone cruelty to animals, one must take into account the progress of science and, indeed, the advancement of society at large. Possibly a substantial fine and perhaps even a few days contemplating the walls of the Cook County Jailhouse will help these women see the error of their actions.

The story was without byline, but I recognized its style and tone. I made a mental note to have a discussion with its author upon returning to Chicago.

I tossed the paper to the floor. "Well, you've done it this time, Pamela," I said to the empty room. Tomorrow I would send her a telegram; tonight I just wanted to get away from everything. I looked again at the laudanum drops.

After dimming the light, I crawled beneath the covers. Outside, there were sounds of the crew battening down the riverboat against a now fierce wind. It was the kind of steady night gale that often leaves the streets of town shingled nearly as well as the rooftops.

We were moored on the wharf, and yet the riverboat swayed and rolled on the water. I closed my eyes. The rolling reminded me of the time we had taken a clipper around the Horn on our way to California. I could see how a body could get seasick even on a riverboat.

Sleep came only in fits and starts, the kind a frightened child sleeps in a thunderstorm. Dreams came and went with the uneasy sleep. In my imagination, I saw again that vision of Elcid Hardacre standing in the middle of a circle, bird on shoulder. This time, a few new faces were added to those dancing around him—Marshal Thurmond, Nellie Dawes, and Thomas Cooper. I dreamed of other things too—of being chased by someone from my past, and of my mother's funeral. But as the night passed, the dreams took a more pleasant turn. I even envisioned Horace and I making love, and it was a disappointment to awake just before dawn, Horace now at my side, snoring softly, a contented look on his face.

I wondered if . . . But just then a light flickered in the hallway. With the transom window open, I could make out a soft shuffling of feet, as if someone were stealing down the hall. The light seemed to be moving in a left-to-right direction toward Hardacre's room. I was still in that nether world between dreams and dawn, yet my mind registered that the light was too faint for an ordinary lamp and could only be coming from a candle or a dampened lantern.

Presently I heard the sound of metal on metal. A key and a lock? I waited, unsure of what to make of it or what to do next. 'A criminal will often return to the place of a crime.' Probably a Pinkerton adage or maybe even one of his own. In either case, it just might be that this stealthy nightwalker was returning to Hardacre's room, to the scene of his own crime. I considered waking my sleeping husband but decided to investigate on my own. The hallway was quiet now, no light flickering in the pre-dawn darkness. Outside it was quiet too, the storm having gone as quickly as it had come.

Pulling a wooden chair near the door, I found that by raising myself on my toes and holding on to the door frame, I could just see into the corridor. Minutes passed. I listened to Horace's rhythmic snoring, hoping he wouldn't wake to find me standing on a chair, peering foolishly into an empty hallway.

But soon the sound of a key and a lock proved I hadn't imagined the whole thing. Again, the shuffling of feet. This time the sound was coming from the opposite direction. A hand sconce and candle preceded the figure of a man. The light in the corridor was dim, but there could be no mistaking the lanky frame and white hair of Dr. Sidney Cotton. The figure disappeared; a door was opened at the end of the hall, and I thought I heard the muffled sound of voices, one of which sounded like a woman's. A door was closed, leaving me standing tiptoed on the chair, peering into darkness.

THE DECISION OF
THE CHAIR

———◆———

I t has always been Horace's rule to work at two things
at once. "One spends thousands of hours in a lifetime
at simple tasks such as shaving," as he liked to say. "Why
not put those hours to some use?" And so the morning
found Horace engaged in not two, but three activities si-
multaneously. With a lathered face which held a half-
smoked cigarette, he sat staring at the newspaper, and gave
out a low decrescendo whistle. "Have you seen this,
Sadie?" He pointed his straight razor at the paper.

I walked drowsily to his side. "I'm afraid so."

The eyes that looked back at mine were amused.
"Antivivisection League. Really, Sadie, this is a bit much,
even for Pamela."

I had an urge to give him a jab to the arm, but re-
strained myself. He was right; it did seem a bit much.

"Are you going to go back to Chicago to be with her?"

"I was going to send her a telegram this morning, but
I think she'll decline any help."

"Good! Then you can continue to help me. Marshal
Thurmond is a good man, but he has his deficiencies as a
detective."

"And I do not?" I asked.

Horace remained silent—a sort of challenging silence it seemed to me. He pulled out his watch, looked at it, then turned toward the chair I had used the previous night, which still stood in front of the door. For some reason, I chose to remain silent too—about the chair and about what I had seen the night before.

"Nearly seven," he said at last. "I want to check on the young lady across the hall. According to Dr. Cotton, she was in her room when Hardacre was shot. Maybe she heard something." Horace looked again at the door and the chair. "You can hear pretty well what's going on in the hallway from these rooms." He removed the last of the lather with his razor, carefully wiped the blade clean, then snapped the blade shut. "You'd better hurry, Sadie. Thurmond should be here in ten minutes."

I have always found that fasting is good for the imagination, but for clear thinking give me a full stomach. Unfortunately, Horace did not share my philosophy and rarely ate when on a case. After reaching into the recesses of my handbag, I had to content myself with a pair of chocolates and a solitary bulls-eye peppermint. I arranged my confections on the bureau and began preparing myself for the day.

Ten minutes was completely inadequate for this, but I would have to make do. I washed and put on a bottle-blue dress, not altogether subdued in cut but not too showy. In ten minutes the marshal had arrived, and in fifteen we were standing at the door of stateroom F.

"Just a minute," came a voice from inside. The door

opened and a woman looked questioningly, first at all three of our faces, then at the marshal's badge. "Is something wrong?" she asked.

Horace and Thurmond seemed not to hear. They stood staring at her. She couldn't have been much more than twenty. She had the air of a woman who seemed, despite her age, to have endured some great sorrow, an air older men seem to find compelling. Her eyes were striking, yet for some reason seemed remote, a mysterious blue-grey one might expect to see on a far-off mountaintop. But for all that they were also wide and well-decorated, considering the hour. I felt a pinch of jealousy, and wished I'd had more than ten minutes this morning in front of the mirror.

"Yes, there is something wrong," Horace said at last. "May we come in?"

"Of course," she said, ushering us inside. A low-cut plum-colored dress did little to hide her figure.

Her name was Mary Atchison, we were told as Marshal Thurmond made the proper introductions—Miss Mary Atchison. He explained the purpose of our visit while Horace removed his note pad from a breast pocket. After making several notations, he tore off the top sheet and offered it to me solemnly. 'Fat ankles,' the note read, and I relaxed, holding back a smile.

I have a natural inclination for probing, especially when in the room of another woman. I casually studied the room as Horace began his questions: Did she know Hardacre? Had she ever been on the *Mississippi Girl* before? Did she know any passengers or crew? Had she heard anything out of the common last night? All were answered quietly and with one word: No.

I walked noiselessly across the cocoa matting on the floor while listening to her answers. Unfortunately, there was little probing to be done here. The room was nearly devoid of personal items. A shoulder cape hung in an open closet, a sort of Confederate-grey cape coat with shiny silver buttons. A small travel case was open and revealed what appeared to be a drab green sweater under which were several white undergarments. The hat I had admired on the previous day was hung carelessly on a chair, which also held yesterday's dress. Beneath the chair was a pair of button-eye boots of a style out of fashion for nearly five years. Quite a diverse variety of clothing, I thought.

On a night stand were a book, a pair of eye glasses, and an empty bottle of olive oil. The olive oil held my attention for a moment. I wondered what she used it for. If it was used as a night cream, my readers would certainly be interested. I made a mental note to ask her when we were alone. I lifted the book from the night stand and read its title. *Drum-Taps*. Taste in hats, taste in books. I decided not to hold her striking features against her.

"There was a bit of a celebration last night, Miss Atchison," Horace continued. "Did you not hear the shots or the fireworks?"

She thought for a moment. "Now that you mention it . . . I was quite drowsy, you see, but I may have heard something of the sort while in bed; I thought I was dreaming it. I should explain," she said. "I have some difficulty with seasickness when traveling—even on a riverboat. I consulted the old doctor from down the hall, who suggested the best remedy would be sleep. I was told we would be waylaid here for a time, and, as I had no plans for the evening, I took both his advice and an elixir he prepared for me. That must have been just past six, I believe. So I cannot be sure if I heard the shots or merely dreamt of hearing them."

"Most of the celebrating was done below on the middle deck, but we know at least one shot was discharged just across the hall. Do you remember one particularly loud report?"

"I'm sorry I can't be more helpful," she said, shaking her head. "But I just don't recall anything of the kind. Like I said, I'm not altogether certain I heard fireworks and pistol shots at all."

Horace's right hand tapped on a side table, preoccupied it seemed. I fingered my pendant and Thurmond stood by, quietly observing the young woman.

"What is your destination?" Horace asked.

"Home. That is to say, St. Peters. It's a little town just north of St. Louis. I was hoping to get there today." She turned her wide eyes toward Marshal Thurmond. "I will be able to leave today, won't I? My mother is all alone and I'm anxious to get back to her."

"I think we can arrange something, ma'am," he said. When Horace gave him a pointed look, he added, "That is to say, if all goes well with the investigation."

"Do I take it from what you say that you have no suspects?"

"We have a few clues, ma'am. And I'm sure it won't be long till we have our man."

"Or woman," I said, remembering the woman's voice I heard from Dr. Cotton's room. I decided to take advantage of a momentary silence to ask the question that had been on my mind since last night. I also decided to ask it directly, to see if she would be caught off her guard. "Can you tell me why you were in Dr. Cotton's room earlier this morning?"

There was more surprise on the faces of Horace and Thurmond than on the young lady. "This morning?" she said evenly. "I'm sure you must mean last night, when I saw the doctor."

She appeared not in the least taken back by my suggestion. But if it was not her I heard talking with Dr. Cotton, then who? Mrs. DuBois was the only other woman staying on the texas deck. If it was anyone else, she would have been seen by the boys in the pilothouse.

"To tell the truth," I said, pressing the matter, "I was not speaking of last night. I heard Dr. Cotton conversing with someone this morning, and I thought it was you."

Again, her voice was even. "It must have been someone else you heard, Mrs. Greenstreet. I haven't been out of my room since yesterday evening."

What a strange profession it was to be a Pinkerton agent, I thought as I listened to her words. How many times had Horace pried into the affairs of others? How many times had he opened a safe, dusted powder on a floor, or even stood on a chair in the middle of the night?

The smell of smokey pitch pine drifted through the

window. The shrill whistle of a riverboat signaled a departure. I closed my eyes for a time, and imagined myself and Horace aboard. We could be bound for anywhere, as long as it was away from Cairo, away from the *Mississippi Girl,* away from murder.

And yet, as the thought began to fade in my mind, it occurred to me that I was not altogether unhappy being right where I was.

Presently, there was a knock at the door. "Mr. Greenstreet, are you in there?" The voice was that of Allan Culbertson.

Horace opened the door and let in the clerk. "It's the captain," he said. "You wanted to know when he returned, and he's on the wharf now. He dropped off his trunk by the freighter a few slips down, and was making his way toward the *Mississippi Girl.*"

"Tell the captain we wish to see him—in stateroom E. No need to explain why if he doesn't already know," Horace said. Culbertson hesitated at the door.

"Is there something else?"

"Yes. It's the passengers. They're getting restless to get underway. They will have to be told what is going on. Most of the crew knows that Hardacre is dead, and rumors are spreading among the passengers that a murderer is aboard. We'll have to tell them something."

Horace addressed the marshal. "I think you should handle the passengers, Jack. If we don't have answers after we talk to McQuaid, they'll have to be told." He thought for a moment, then said, "In either case, I suspect this riverboat isn't going to finish its journey to St. Louis, and those aboard will have to make other arrangements."

As the clerk left the room, I thought it odd that, unlike Horace and the marshal, he hadn't shown the least interest in Miss Atchison. Not once had he even looked her way.

"I trust you will let us know if anything further comes to mind, Miss Atchison," Horace said.

She struck me as being preoccupied and answered without much emotion. "Yes, I'll be sure to do that," she said.

RETURN OF THE CAPTAIN

———◆———

I was feeling a touch of guilt for not telling Horace what I'd seen last night. And as time passed I knew it would become more and more difficult to do so. He would have to be told eventually, but I wanted to speak with Dr. Cotton alone. Maybe there was a good explanation for his actions. Maybe, though I was beginning to doubt it.

Horace and the marshal exchanged a few words, moved three chairs from Hardacre's room to stateroom E, and took up positions near two of the chairs. I waited on the edge of the large bed. I remembered I was still hungry, having not eaten breakfast, but again the picture of the woman over the bedstead kept me from my chocolates.

I looked up and saw Captain McQuaid standing in the doorway. He was in full uniform, blue pants and a jacket cut tight at the shoulders, which bore some sort of maritime insignia. He was newly shaven and his black hair was combed straight back and appeared slightly wet. When he spoke, there was surliness in his voice.

"What's this about a wife and child? Who's pulling my leg?"

Horace and the marshal turned in my direction.

"I'm afraid it was necessary," I said. "If I had revealed the real reasons we wished to speak to you, it is likely you wouldn't have come. Besides, the man at the union hall didn't appear the type to keep a murder under his hat." This was only half the truth, I knew. I had lied to the man at the union hall mostly because I wanted to impress the young cub pilot. "Hardacre is dead," I said.

"Dead?" He looked at Horace, then the marshal, then shrugged. "Too bad," he said, without conviction. "But that's no concern of mine. You see, I don't work for him anymore."

"But it does concern you," Horace said. "It concerns you if it was you that killed him."

Captain McQuaid took a step forward. He was an imposing figure, standing nearly a head taller than Horace. "Are you accusing me of murder?" he said.

Horace's face and his voice expressed no opinion as he pointed to a chair. "Sit down, Captain McQuaid, and I will tell you how things stand."

McQuaid sat himself down carefully, both hands squeezing the wooden arms. Horace moved closer, standing now at least a head taller than McQuaid. He said, "Hardacre was last seen just before you left the *Mississippi Girl*. He was probably shot at about the same time of the commotion on the deck below." The captain's eyes were immobile as Horace circled the chair. "You went to a lot of trouble, pulling up from the dock and running out to where the rivers meet. A flamboyant thing to do, especially the fireworks. And how convenient it should occur—just as if someone planned the thing so no one could hear the firing of one more pistol."

McQuaid's big hands continued to clutch the arms of the chair, his voice seemed strained. "It's a thing I've done for years," he said. "I guess I'm fond of giving that speech, and the passengers always seem to like it. You see, there was a position open on the freighter *Northern Star*, so I thought this might be my last run on a showboat. I figured I might as well give it one more time. Besides, I knew it would get under Hardacre's skin, especially when he found I'd left the riverboat." Captain McQuaid fixed his eyes on the open door to Hardacre's room. "But as for the celebrating that took place afterwards, I can't say I planned it, or even had anything to do with it."

Horace pulled out his tobacco pouch, then changed his mind and returned it to his pocket. He said, "Possibly it was spontaneous, but that's not to say you didn't take advantage of the situation."

The captain's face had a reddish cast, slightly blotchy at the cheeks. He held his chin out in the pose a man takes when daring another to land a blow. He drew in, then expelled a deep breath. "So you *are* accusing me of murder."

"That will be up to Marshal Thurmond," Horace said. "The evidence, so far, is indirect. But as of now we know of only a handful of people who were in a position to commit the murder."

McQuaid and the lawman leveled gazes on one another. The captain's eyes were the color of gunpowder tea, slightly glazed now, like a prizefighter who had just taken a punch. Thurmond's gaze was noncommittal. He was perfectly content to let Horace do the questioning. And, unlike other lawmen I'd known, he wasn't the sort who let the power of his position go to his head. I had to admire him for that.

"I should have known I couldn't walk away from Hardacre and his riverboat that easy," the captain said. He shook his head and whispered beneath his breath, "Damn luck."

Horace resumed his inquiry. "Let us assume, for the sake of argument, that you are telling the truth and did not kill Hardacre. When you returned from the saloon to your stateroom, did you notice anything unusual?"

"I can't say as I did. Like I said, there was talk of an open billet aboard a freighter, and I was anxious to get ashore and get myself to the union hall. I was already packed, and I only stayed in my room a short time before I went ashore. Mr. Bixby can vouch for that. He came down from the pilothouse and helped me with my trunk."

"Who else knew you were leaving?" Horace asked.

"Only Mr. Culbertson. I asked him earlier to have my wages sent on to the shipping office in St. Paul. Though I can't say I expected Hardacre to pay me after leaving without notice." McQuaid paused, then looked up. "As a matter of fact, it was Culbertson who suggested I take the boat out and give my speech one more time."

Horace pulled out a square-headed nail and showed it to the captain. "Do you recognize this?"

McQuaid took the nail, rolled it over in his hand, and

returned it to Horace. "It looks like one of mine," he said. "But I can't be sure."

"It is almost certainly yours, Captain McQuaid. You will notice the small amount of tobacco tar at the tip of the nail, showing it was used to clean a pipe."

"Then it is my nail. What of it?"

"It was found on the floor near Hardacre's body."

The captain thought about that, then laughed. It was a hollow laugh, a laugh without mirth or even emotion. He brought out two similar nails from a pocket. "You will find these all over the boat. I have this careless habit of leaving them lying about. It wouldn't surprise me at all if one of them ended up in Hardacre's room."

"That may be, but Mrs. Dawes cleaned the room earlier in the day. She claims it was not on the floor then." Horace circled the captain's chair a second time. "When was the last time you were in Hardacre's room?"

McQuaid thought for a moment, "I guess the day before yesterday."

Horace thrust both hands into his trouser pockets and said, "On which side did you fight during the war?"

"I was too old for conscription, but my sentiments were with the Unionists."

"What kind of gun do you own?" Horace asked.

"You'll find a Sharpes long rifle in my trunk, nothing smaller."

"I'd like to take a look at that trunk, Captain McQuaid. Do I need a key?"

The captain shook his head. "Naw. It's held shut with a couple of straps and buckles."

Marshal Thurmond brushed his twill weave jacket. Looking up, he found Horace staring at him. "I'm going to take a look in that trunk," Horace said. "You may as well clear the boat of passengers and unneeded crew. It might be a good idea to call in an undertaker to take away the body." He checked his pocket watch, giving its silver stem a few turns, then turned toward me. "See what you can find in Hardacre's safe, Sadie. Let's see just who stands to gain from his death."

Thurmond raked a large right hand through his hair. "What should we do with him?" he said, pointing at the captain.

"You're the marshal," Horace said, shrugging.

Thurmond thought about that, then said to McQuaid, "You are advised to remain on board and in your room till this matter is settled."

McQuaid roared up from his chair, his hands clenched and shaking slightly. Before he could speak, the marshal showed the man his own fist. "You quarreled with the man," he said, raising a forefinger. "You created a diversion to cover the sound of a bullet." A second finger was raised. "You were here in the upper deck about the time he was killed." Another finger. "You left the boat in a hurry and found employment on another steamer." Thurmond let several seconds pass before extending a final finger. "And one of your nails is found lying near Hardacre's body.

"Now I don't know if you killed the man or not— that's for a judge to decide. But I'd say we've enough here to make a pretty strong case you did." Captain McQuaid fell back into his chair. "I'll let the pilot on the *Northern Star* know how things stand," Thurmond continued. Then he addressed Horace, "Anything else?"

"Only the suggestion that we gather everyone together in the saloon in, say, two hours. Sadie can give us the details of Hardacre's will at that time. I'm not certain what is to be gained, but I've always found that a confrontation brings out the worst in people. If one questions their innocence, they have a tendency to say things about each other that may not be said if alone."

As we left the room, each to our tasks, a curious thing happened in the hallway. Wearing a primrose dress and no apron, Nellie Dawes was standing in front of Dr. Cotton's door, holding a tray of tea and buttered scones. Presently, the doctor opened the door.

The chambermaid appeared discomposed, as she said in an unnecessarily loud voice, "Here is the tea you ordered, Dr. Cotton. Do you wish to have your room cleaned now?"

"Don't clean the rooms just yet," Horace interrupted. "Make the beds if you want to, and bring something to eat for the captain and anyone else who doesn't want to go below, but don't touch anything else in the rooms just yet."

The chambermaid set down her tray on a table just inside Dr. Cotton's room. "And one more thing," Horace said, still addressing her. "Tell everyone on this deck to meet in the saloon in two hours."

"Does that include me?" she asked.

"Yes," I answered before Horace could. He looked at me queerly, but said nothing, and we broke up into four directions—Captain McQuaid to his room, the marshal and Horace toward the outer door, and Nellie Dawes down the hall. As for me, I followed the food into Dr. Cotton's room. "I have a headache, Dr. Cotton," I said. "May I come in?"

"Yes, by all means, sit down and I'll see what I can do for you."

DR. COTTON'S
STATEROOM

———◆·◆·◆———

D
r. Cotton's quarters were much as one would expect from a bachelored old man of science. Medical books, folios, and experimental apparatus were strewn
haphazardly about the room. Jars of ointments, liquids,
and powders were mingled among them, exuding a mixture of pungent and subtle odors, mostly of volatile oils and
spirits. I examined the labels on the various medicines.
Some bore exotic names—cascara sagrada, oil of gaulthe-
ria, nux vomica. Others had labels with names more mun-
dane—leeches, sulfur and molasses, rosewater.

As I took in the rest of the room, something about it
struck me as odd, yet I couldn't say just what. A large cen-
tral table held a carved wooden chess set, with pieces in
place as if waiting for a game. The chess set and table were
both oversized, and seemed to hold command over the entire room. Old newspapers were draped across cane-
backed chairs and piled into uneven stacks. On the far
wall were a pair of surgical saws, crossed as if they were
fencing sabres. I smiled to myself, noticing the peanut
shells littering the floor. There was not a bed in the room,

but a wide divan with a blue coverlet and pillows indicated where Dr. Cotton slept.

Then it struck me. The disorder only applied to the right side of the room. To the left, on the divan side, the floor had been swept, furniture polished and, showing the touch of a woman, a vase of wildflowers adorned a side table.

"You only allow her to clean half your room," I said, while taking a chair.

"I beg your pardon."

"I mean Mrs. Dawes. She only tends to half the room."

He looked at me cautiously, and smiled a guarded smile. A pouch of tobacco rotated from one cheek to the other before he answered. "Well, I guess I like things just so and so does she. This may look like disorder to you, but I know where everything is." He proved his point by pulling a bottle of smelling camphor from a cluttered shelf and handing it to me. "Will this do," he asked, "or would you like something stronger?"

"Oh yes, the headache," I said, remembering why I had come. "Perhaps if I just had some of the tea and biscuits Mrs. Dawes left you it would go away. Isn't it fortunate she came with two cups on the tray?" I held the bottle in my lap and watched the old physician as he retrieved the tray and placed it near me.

He took a chair across from me and studied my face for a time as I poured the tea and took a bite of a biscuit. He said, "I take it this call wasn't entirely a professional one."

"As a matter of fact, there is something troubling me."

I looked again at the side table and the wildflowers. "Does she often spend the night?" I asked.

For the first time since I'd met the man, he became flustered. He coughed a nervous cough. "Mrs. Greenstreet, you surprise me. I realize you are assisting your husband with his inquiries, but really, that isn't the kind of question I expected from your lips."

I smoothed a wrinkle on my dress then, setting aside the camphor said, "It's just that I heard you speaking with a woman very early this morning. That was right after you paid your visit to Hardacre's room." Either my words had had a profound effect on him, or perhaps he had just swallowed his tobacco—perhaps both, I could not say for certain. He coughed again, then spit into a metal cuspidor.

His eyes refused to meet mine, but at length he lifted his head. "What makes you think it was Mrs. Dawes?"

"Two cups on the serving tray, for one thing," I said. "The other is this room. It is obviously a compromise."

He gave me an interrogative raise of the forehead. "A compromise?"

"Yes. She must spend some time here, as this side of the room is neat and shows a woman's touch. The other side looks like a magpie's nest, so it is likely she compromised and lets you keep that side as you would have it. Now I can't say for certain if the voice I heard last night was hers, but you don't compromise with a maid, unless she is more than just that."

Dr. Cotton squinted his eyes, as if he were trying to see

me more clearly. "And you say I made a visit to Hardacre's room?"

"That, I'm afraid, is not speculation. You see, I watched you steal down the hallway last night."

"You already know about five-eighths of the story," he said in his precise manner. "I'll own up and make things right if you'll promise not to tell your husband or the marshal."

"You know I can't do that," I protested.

"I don't guess you can, but I'll leave it to you just the same. Yesterday, when we met outside the saloon, I had just won a considerable amount of money. But my luck hasn't always been that good. The fact of the matter is, lately I've more often than not ended up on the losing end.

"Hardacre kept a ledger, and in it a tally of what I owed." The old physician moved uneasily in his chair. "It amounted to nearly a thousand dollars. And when Hardacre died . . . Well, let's just say that Hardacre didn't have any relatives, so far as I know. I just thought it would be a shame to have my debts still on his books." He paused and looked at me plaintively.

"So you removed the ledger from his room," I said.

Dr. Cotton shook his head. "Not the ledger, just the page listing my debts." His voice was a subdued monotone.

"May I see it?" I asked.

"I'm afraid I burned it." Again he coughed, then continued in his doctoral manner, though I noticed a bead of sweat forming on his forehead. "Where was I going to get nine hundred and sixty dollars?"

It seemed the world was full of social bandits, I mused. Rob from the rich and give to the poor. And if it is you yourself that is poor, then by all means keep the money and omit the middle man. I couldn't condemn the practice, for it was exactly how Horace and I had survived so many years ago. I said, "And it was Mrs. Dawes who supplied you with the key to Hardacre's room."

Dr. Cotton nodded.

"And it was she who I heard in your room."

"It was. But it was my idea entirely, not hers," he added quickly. "She only did as I asked."

I thought a man capable of stealing from a dead man might also be capable of lying. "Are you quite certain of the time of death?" I asked.

He gave me an offended look, as if I were questioning his integrity. It was an unusual response to say the least, considering his position. "The time of Hardacre's death was just past six," he said flatly.

I munched absent-mindedly on my breakfast, considering what to do next. "Why didn't you tell us of Mr. Hardacre's medical condition?" I asked.

"That was a confidential matter, Mrs. Greenstreet. Besides, I didn't see the import of it."

"How long did he have?"

The doctor hesitated. "Well, things as they are, I don't suppose confidentiality matters much now. I'd estimate he had two, maybe three months to live. Hard to tell with these things. He had a condition of the heart, a congestive condition not helped much by his habit of drinking two bottles of fortified wine every day." Dr. Cotton paused, his face now hard. His dove-grey eyes were clear and wide. "You may think I had something to do with his death, Mrs. Greenstreet, considering the money I owed. But why would I kill a man who was going to die anyway? And as long as Hardacre was alive, at least I had a chance to win it back."

I continued to question Dr. Cotton for a minute or two, and as I did I was aware of an uneasy feeling creeping into my mind. It seemed to me I was overlooking some point. There was more to this than there appeared on the surface. But what? Someone among the passengers and crew was lying. But who? And whether it was for my own vanity or because of a rivalry with Horace, I knew I wanted to piece together what really had happened.

I concluded my interview with Dr. Cotton and made my way toward Hardacre's room. In the hallway, I again met Nellie Dawes. She barely gave me a glance as she quickly passed by, her face flushed and her eyes excited. But she had the presence of mind to continue her charade. "May I come in and take away your breakfast?" I heard her say at Dr. Cotton's open door. The doctor murmured something I couldn't make out, then she entered and closed the door.

Nellie Dawes had told us earlier that she was in her room at the time of the murder. I wondered if anyone could verify her story. Further down the hallway, I stood before the door of stateroom F, the room of the young lady named Atchison who suffered from seasickness. I wondered about her, too. She certainly was not suffering any ill effects this morning. I considered knocking at her door and asking about the olive oil on her nightstand, but there was not time for that now. Instead, I turned my attention to compartment G and the will in Elcid Hardacre's safe.

XVIII

A Will, a Letter, a Promise

———◆———

With the key supplied by Mr. Culbertson in hand, I entered the room of the late Elcid Hardacre. It was an eerie feeling, entering the room of a dead man, especially now that I was alone. For some reason I cannot explain, I found myself tiptoeing past the body. After memorizing the date of the elder Hardacre's death, I pulled down his picture and opened the combination safe. I found a bag filled with gold coins, all minted in Sacramento; a stack of bank notes, most printed by the Planter's Bank of St. Louis; and two bottles of very old Napoleon brandy. Near the back of the safe was the will, rolled tightly and tied with a red ribbon.

Old habits die slowly; after a moment I left the bank notes be, limiting myself to the will, a single twenty-dollar gold piece, and one unopened bottle of brandy. After all, they might be evidence, I thought, as I slipped the three items into my handbag. As I prepared to leave, I noticed a small painting of an epic scene. At the center of the picture, a pope dressed in a blood-red robe stood pointing, I supposed, toward Jerusalem. With him, a man who may have been King Richard (his grey horse wore a symbolic red cross on a white background) led an army of rag-tag men. Another group of devilish-looking men pointed and jeered at those being led off to war. It was unlike anything else in the room, and especially out-of-keeping with Hardacre's mercantile philosophy. The picture and the question which went with it lingered in my mind like an unwanted tune. What significance could such a painting have for a man like Hardacre?

Returning to my own compartment, I heard the sound of voices coming from the room of Mary Atchison. I put my ear to the door. Although I couldn't make out the words, the voices were speaking to each other in an agitated manner. What was unmistakable, however, was the timbre of those voices—one was undoubtedly masculine and the other feminine. I waited by the door for a long moment, unsure of what to do or what to make of it. It might have nothing at all to do with the case, and yet I was curious to know who was visiting Miss Atchison. If someone had come up from the deck below, then whoever was manning the pilothouse would have noticed. Otherwise, it could only be one of three men: Dr. Cotton, Andrew DuBois, or Mr. Culbertson. I resolved to use some stealth in finding out.

I retrieved the bottle of fuller's earth from Horace's Pinkerton bag, spreading a thin layer of the powder at the threshold of Miss Atchison's door. I was rather pleased with my handiwork, having used Horace's methods to appease my curiosity.

As I returned to my compartment, the sound of horse and wheels, as well as voices, drew me to my window. I watched the outgoing flow of people leaving the *Mississippi Girl*. Marshal Thurmond stood at the side of the gang-planks, checking off the names of passengers from a roster. In the opposite direction, a tall man dressed in a black suit and black undertaker's hat led two other men aboard. The two men were carrying a long pine box.

Darting to and fro among barrels stacked further down the wharf, I watched a brown swallow. It put me in mind of the European starling my mother kept in a bedroom cage

so many years ago. She suffered with a condition the doctors called melancholy and mania, a condition I often fear I may have inherited. When her mood was especially grey, she would sit alone in her bed and watch and talk to that bird for hours on end.

When my mother died, I opened that birdcage and let the starling fly away. But the bird never would stray far, choosing instead to return to the safety of that cage. These last few years, I felt myself becoming more and more like that starling, each of us a homebody, straying less and less from home.

Unlike my mother, whose mania lasted for days and melancholy for months, my own version of the malady often saw these changes occur two or three times a day. I felt a sudden urge to return to my home in Chicago, to the security of my books and my easy chair. And Horace would understand if I did.

It even occurred to me that this whole affair had been orchestrated by Horace and Pamela to get me away from my sedentary life. Both had often remarked that a change would do me good. If they had plotted to get me away, surely they couldn't have foreseen that a leisurely trip on a showboat would end in murder.

I found one of Horace's half-smoked cigarettes in a receptacle and lit it carefully. As I drew in a deep breath, I tried to rid my mind of melancholy thoughts of home and starlings. "Pull yourself together, Sadie," I said to my reflection in a highboy mirror. "Clear thinking is what's needed here. You promised you would help Horace, not be a burden."

When I had finished the cigarette I felt more relaxed. I reached in my bag and found one of the bulls-eye peppermints I always took after pilfering Horace's cigarettes. After untying the string and breaking the seal on Hardacre's will, I sat down on the side of my bed to read it.

The will was written in a very precise hand on thick bleached parchment paper. The paper was fairly new, I judged, probably less than a year old. This was confirmed as I looked at the bottom of the document and found it dated March 23, 1873. Under the heading of the Planter's Bank of St. Louis was the following:

Last Will and Testament
of
Elcid J. Hardacre

I, Elcid J. Hardacre of the City of St. Louis and State of Missouri, being of sound and disposing mind and memory and well realizing the objects of my bounty, do hereby make this my Last Will and Testament and I hereby revoke all former wills and testamentary dispositions heretofore at any time made by me.

Article I

I hereby appoint the Planter's Bank of St. Louis as executor of my estate and I authorize and direct said executor to sell any and all property that I may own at the time of my decease, including my three steamboats which I own outright, for the purpose of raising funds to pay the legacies mentioned in this Will.

And as for payment of services to be rendered in the administration of this Last Will and Testament, I give and bequeath to the Planter's Bank of St. Louis the sum of One Thousand dollars.

Article II

I give and bequeath to Nellie Dawes, who has long been in the employ of my family, the sum of Two Thousand dollars.

Article III

I hereby release and absolutely discharge my personal physician, Sidney M. Cotton, from all debts which he may owe me or may be construed to owe me at the time of my decease. Said indebtedness is recorded on page seventeen of the *Mississippi Girl* official ledger.

I paused and reflected on this bit of irony. Doctor Cotton had stolen page seventeen from the ledger, a page now rendered worthless by Hardacre's own words. I continued.

Article IV

The remainder of my estate, in its entirety, I hereby give and bequeath to the Union Soldier's Home of St. Louis, Missouri, to be used for the care and comfort of its residents.

IN WITNESS WHEREOF, I have hereunto set my hand this twenty-third day of March in the year of our Lord eighteen hundred and seventy-three.

ELCID J. HARDACRE

"This is odd." Again I was addressing my reflection in the mirror. "What connection did Hardacre have to a soldier's home in St. Louis?" I was reminded of the statement from the chambermaid stating that Hardacre was not a soldier and was sent away to England when the war broke out.

Feeling the seed of a solution taking hold in my mind, I removed a chocolate from my reticule and began to pace the floor nervously. Five minutes passed, along with two more chocolates, before I gave it up and embarked on a new tack. I have found that it is often wise to put down thoughts on paper and so make them more clear in your mind.

I went to the writing desk and took up my pen.

> My dear Pamela—
>
> Your designs, if they were designs, to get me out of the house have been successful. Let me tell you of the remarkable events which have taken place since leaving Chicago . . .

I continued my narrative, telling of the various circumstances and events. I wrote nearly two pages of my thoughts concerning the death of Elcid Hardacre, when I was startled by a knock at the door.

Opening the door, I found Thomas Cooper staring at

 me like a face from the past. He removed the leather-billed cap from his head. "May I—may I come in?" he stammered.

"Of course. Come in," I indicated to one of the high-backed chairs.

I offered him a chocolate, but he declined and said, "I thought I should tell you about Mrs. Dawes."

"Mrs. Dawes?"

"I didn't tell you about it because, well, it's embarrassing, two people their age." He shuffled his feet nervously.

"You mean Mrs. Dawes and Dr. Cotton?"

"Yes. You asked who was on the texas when Mr. Hardacre got murdered. I didn't mention it because I didn't think it important, but maybe it is. You see, Mrs. Dawes usually brings the doctor his supper and then stays for an hour or two. I didn't see her come up yesterday evening because my shift didn't start till six. But a few minutes after six, I saw Dr. Cotton leaving, and about a quarter hour later she came down." He paused for a moment, brushing back a wisp of hair from his forehead and looking at me sidewise to get my reaction.

"That is their habit, you know," he continued. "One leaves the room and the other waits for a time so they aren't seen leaving together. But everyone knows about them anyways."

"You're quite sure about the time?" I asked.

"Oh, yes. She came down just after we made our swing out on the Mississippi."

"Had the fireworks and pistol shots begun?"

He thought for a moment then shook his head. "I can't say for certain. Is it important?"

"Probably," I said. "One of the shots killed Mr. Hardacre."

"Like I say, I can't be certain. But you don't think she shot him, do you?"

"My husband says you should always suspect everyone. But enough talk about that. I want to know what your plans are. Will you be able to find work on another steamboat?"

"I talked to Mr. Bixby in the pilothouse this morning. He says that pilot's work will be hard to find on the river. But I've got enough money saved and I've decided to try my luck in San Francisco."

I felt a touch of sorrow upon hearing this news. "What will you do there?"

Thomas Cooper shrugged. "Work on the wharf or maybe aboard an ocean packet. Mr. Bixby wrote me a letter of introduction."

I went to the writing desk and wrote down an address. "You must see Mrs. Finch. She runs a boardinghouse on Polk Street. A respectable place. And you must promise you'll stay clear of the Waterfront District. That part of town isn't suitable for a young man."

I sounded like a mother, I knew, but he didn't seem to mind and gave me a toothy grin. "I promise," he said as I gave him the paper. He seemed unsure of what to do next, but settled with a firm handshake.

"One more thing before you go," I said.

I retrieved the twenty-dollar gold piece and placed it in his hand. "I am a great believer in luck charms," I said. "Keep this with you to remember me and your time on the *Mississippi Girl.*"

He pocketed the coin and letter, placed his cap on his head, and smiling, reached for the door. "I hope you find the murderer," he said.

I stood there, unconsciously rubbing my cat's-eye pendant as I listened to the sounds of his metal boot cleats retreating down the hallway. When I could no longer hear them, I returned to my writing desk and my letter to Pamela.

> I feel my journey has taken me further than just Cincinnati or Cairo. Again, that may be just as you had hoped for. I find myself thinking less of the past and more of the future, or at least the present.
>
> The case is currently at an impasse. Although, as you can see, all the facts point to Captain McQuaid, I am not so certain.
>
> Now that I have conveyed to you the events surrounding the murder on the *Mississippi Girl,* I must turn to you, Pamela, for I've heard of your little escapade at the house of Dr. Milton. Mr. Tengvall's article in the *Tribune* was not very flattering to you and your group.
>
> I know you are not in the habit of taking ad-

vice, so I will only say this: Be careful and try to stay out of trouble's way until I return. If you are in need of anything, do not hesitate to wire me in care of the Cairo Telegraph Office.

Love,
S.A.G.

XIX

DEATH IN
STATEROOM H

———◆·◆·◆———

As I stepped out into the corridor, intent on mailing Pamela's letter, I heard a woman scream, followed by a crashing sound. It was less a scream than a pained cry—a death cry, shrill and very unsettling.

I couldn't make out the precise direction, but it seemed to have come from either stateroom F or H. Opening the door to compartment F, I found Miss Atchison on the edge of her bed with an open book in hand. "Is something wrong?" she asked in a calm voice.

I did not answer, but rushed to the adjoining stateroom. There I found Allan Culbertson bending over the body of a woman. We stared at each other for a long moment. His cheeks were hot with excitement, his eyes wide and alarmed. She gave out a low guttural sound from somewhere deep within her, an eerie, unearthly sound as if her soul were straining to escape with her last breath. A side table was overturned and a cup broken on the floor.

"She must have had a seizure, an attack of some sort."

I ran to her side as the purser turned his face toward

us. The woman's mouth was open, her features now unmoving as if frozen in a paroxysm of pain. It was the face of the chambermaid, Nellie Dawes.

I drew out a hand mirror from my reticule and, holding the back of her head with a shaking hand, positioned it in front of her mouth. My mind retreated as a vague remembrance and an uneasy feeling began stirring within me.

In the days before my son Thomas died I had sat with him for hours on end, and each time he closed his eyes I would take out my hand mirror to see if the end had come. "Is she dead?" I heard Culbertson's voice as if from some distance away. He repeated his words, and as I looked at his face it appeared to slip slightly out of focus, along with the rest of the room. I was holding my pendant, just as I had when my Thomas died. In a moment, though, my eyes refocused and the room returned as it was.

"Fetch Dr. Cotton, and have him bring his bag," I said.

By now, the room was filled with onlookers—Mary Atchison, Mr. and Mrs. Dubois, and Captain McQuaid. I shouted orders to all, in a voice which surprised me with its command. "Someone get Horace and the marshal. If you can't find them, tell the pilot to sound his whistle till they come. Quick now, help me get her to the bed."

Presently Dr. Cotton entered and, placing his hand on her neck, made the pronouncement I knew was inevitable. His face held a pained grimace, a grim echo of the death-grin of Mrs. Dawes. I never realized how alike was the expression of agony to a smile. When he spoke, it was in a low monotone, as if all his emotions had been extinguished.

"She's dead," the old doctor said very softly as the pilot-house whistle began to sound long and loud for the better part of a minute.

By the time Horace and Marshall Thurmond had arrived, Dr. Cotton had completed a cursory examination. Despite his obvious grief, he proceeded with almost puppet-like precision, examining first her mouth and eyes, then the broken tea cup, and finally the untouched cup of tea, which Culbertson indicated was his.

"Poisoned," he declared at last.

Someone let out a low whistle. Horace stepped over the overturned table, then side-stepped the body like a knight crossing obliquely over a pawn. He knelt near the dead woman and the doctor. "You are quite certain?" he asked.

"I'm afraid there can be no doubt about it. The scent of bitter almond is still on her lips—the unmistakable scent of prussic acid, presumably from that same bottle which was stolen from my room and found its way to Hardacre's. The poison that killed her came from the broken cup you see on the floor, but you should know that the other cup contains poison as well." He was holding her hand now, and for the first time his voice showed emotion. "You will get to the bottom of this, Mr. Pinkerton man." It sounded like an order.

Horace directed a piercing look in Culbertson's direction. "What happened here? What was she doing in your room?"

"She asked if she could come by to discuss what was to be done now that Hardacre was dead and if I thought positions would be offered to the staff by whomever bought the *Mississippi Girl*."

"Were you in the habit of discussing such things with her?"

"As a matter of fact, no. But I am, after all, the purser, and I am privy to much of what goes on aboard this riverboat."

"Can you think of someone aboard who might want to see her dead?" Horace asked.

Culbertson shook his head. "No. But I think you are making a hasty assumption. The poison could well have been meant for me."

"That is doubtful," Dr. Cotton said with a note of combat in his voice. "This tea is a variety of fenugreek which I prescribed for Nellie to aid her digestion. And I must be quite frank. Nellie did not care much for you, Mr. Culbertson, so I find it difficult to believe she would come to you for advice."

Horace played with the side whiskers which hung parenthetically from either side of his face. "I take it this tea—fenugreek, you say—was not commonly served to the passengers and crew?"

"No. To my knowledge, she was the only person aboard who took it."

Horace thought for a moment. "I don't think we ever established where Mrs. Dawes was when Hardacre was shot."

His statement seemed to be directed at no one in particular, so when no one replied, I said, "Mrs. Dawes was on the texas deck when Hardacre was killed. To be more precise, she was in the doctor's room."

"It's true," Dr. Cotton said after a hesitation. "She stayed in my room for a time when I went down to the saloon. It is also possible that she suspected someone or saw something. If she did, she didn't tell me who or what, but she did mention that it was quite possible that the death of Hardacre might work out to her advantage. I didn't press her on the point, but I had the distinct impression she was keeping something from me."

"Maybe she killed Hardacre," Culbertson said. "When she realized she would be found out, she poisoned herself."

"If that were the case, why would she come to your room to do it? And why does your cup also contain poison? No, I think we can safely say she was murdered." Horace's eyes surveyed the room, searching, it seemed, for something. More than anything else, he was searching for answers.

Marshal Thurmond took a step forward and spoke for the first time. "Under the circumstances, shouldn't we postpone our meeting in the saloon?"

"No," Horace said. "If the doctor is up to the task, I would like to go ahead as scheduled."

Doctor Cotton rose on wobbly legs, then righted himself with his cane. Death, which came so easily to the old war doctor, did not come so easily today. "I am at your disposal," he said in a raspy voice. "Like I said before, you're the Pinkerton man—and I leave it to you to get to the bottom of this."

As we filed out of stateroom H, Horace took Marshal Thurmond to one side. They spoke for some time, Horace doing most of the talking, while Thurmond nodded in acknowledgment.

XX

READING
OF A LEGACY

———◆———

W e gathered in the saloon at the appointed hour. Chairs were arranged in a half circle, all facing the green billiard table. From left to right were Dr. Cotton, Mr. Culbertson, with Mr. and Mrs. DuBois in the center, followed by Captain McQuaid and Mary Atchison. Marshal Thurmond was conspicuous by his absence. On the pool table, also arranged in a fan-shape, were six balls—a red, yellow, green, blue, purple, and orange, each seemingly set up to correspond to one of the suspects.

Horace slowly walked around the table, looking one by one at the faces of his six guests. Dr. Cotton's face was tired and drawn, the resigned face of a gambler who had had his bluff called. Captain McQuaid appeared stoic; Mr. DuBois and his wife each reflected a confident, detached air.

Mr. Culbertson and Miss Atchison were more difficult to read, although the former's left boot tapped the floor impatiently. I studied Mary Atchison's features for some time as she gazed straight ahead, her eyes seemingly focused on some distant object.

She wore a lavender dress similar to the one she had

worn the previous day. It was a simple muslin dress with a gathered bodice, probably made by her own hand. That, and the fact she wore no jewelry, gave an indication of her social class. It occurred to me that she was not a wealthy woman, yet here she was, taking passage in a first-class berth on an expensive showboat. She closed her blue eyes for a time as one who is having a trying day, then opened them to look again into some vague emptiness. She, like Mrs. DuBois, wore no headgear today.

Horace pulled out his tobacco pouch, spreading flakes carefully and evenly on a paper, then ran his tongue across its surface. He scratched a wax vesta, lit his cigarette, and clearing his throat, began.

"I believe one or more of you has committed the murders of Elcid Hardacre and Nellie Dawes. It is quite possible that Mr. Hardacre left us a clue before he died. But before we proceed, I think it would be advisable if we read Hardacre's will. It has been my experience that there are three motivations for murder—love, revenge, and money. Let us see who benefits from Hardacre's death."

Horace blew out a plume of smoke while twirling his side-whiskers with a thumb and forefinger. He caught my eye and made signals I took to mean he wanted me to read Hardacre's will.

I stood before the assemblage and read the document, pausing at intervals to look at the faces of the six suspects. When I had finished, Horace said, "This is how I see it. If there is only one man involved in these murders, then the process of elimination says that man is Captain McQuaid.

"My room was broken into on our first day out—

broken into by someone who wished to know my business. During that visit several Pinkerton papers were stolen, along with a letter addressed to Mr. Hardacre which warned him of his impending death. Now, it seems likely this thief is the same person who wrote Mr. Hardacre two threatening notes, one delivered in St. Louis and one in Cincinnati. This Cincinnati letter is the one that was taken from my room. Whoever rifled through the room had a key, and only four people had such a key—Hardacre himself, Captain McQuaid, Nellie Dawes, and Mr. Culbertson. I would add Dr. Cotton to the list also, considering his relationship with Mrs. Dawes. Further, all five were in St. Louis and Cincinnati and could have had the notes delivered to Hardacre.

"At this point, I am inclined to agree with Dr. Cotton when he says the murder of Hardacre took place at some time from just past six, when he was last seen, to about six-thirty. Only three people were in their staterooms during this time: Miss Atchison, Captain McQuaid, and Mrs. Dawes, who was in Dr. Cotton's compartment.

"According to Dr. Cotton, Miss Atchison would have been in no condition to commit a murder. That leaves the chambermaid and the captain. With Mrs. Dawes dead, that leaves only Captain McQuaid.

"On the other hand, if two people were involved, it could mean the chambermaid was acting for someone else who later killed her to make certain she would never tell.

"Mr. Culbertson. Let's begin with you. The murder of Hardacre depends on the fact that a commotion outside the saloon masked the fatal shot from inside his stateroom. I understand that it was you who orchestrated the celebration."

"Well, I did tell the boys to whoop it up a bit. You see, I knew Captain McQuaid was leaving, and I thought we should give him a proper send-off."

"Who else knew of your plan?" Horace asked.

"Only a few deck hands. No one in this room knew, if that's what you mean."

Horace paged through his notebook. "You say you took the position of purser about three months past."

"That is correct."

"Where did you work before that?"

"I worked in a St. Louis bank."

I gave Horace a significant glance. He took my cue and walked slowly toward me. As he rested his left hand on the back of my chair, I pointed nonchalantly to the letterhead of Hardacre's will. Horace's eyesight was not so keen as it once was, and I couldn't be sure if he could read the writing.

Returning to his previous position he picked up the yellow pool ball and said, "You worked for the Planter's Bank?"

Culbertson gave him a surprised turn of the head. "I don't believe I mentioned which bank," he said, then added somewhat carelessly, "But you are again correct; that was the bank."

"Curious," Horace said. "That is the very bank where Elcid Hardacre did his business."

Culbertson shrugged. "Not so very curious. Hardacre

had business dealings with the bank, and we met on several occasions. When I found out he had a position aboard the *Mississippi Girl,* we discussed it and came to an agreement."

"Did you help in drafting this will?" Horace said.

"No. Today is the first I heard of it."

Horace turned the pool ball over in his hand, then sent it into a corner pocket. "Do you know how to use a typing machine?"

"I do, though I can't say I am very good at it."

Horace turned his attention to the purple pool ball, and then Captain McQuaid. "Were you aware of Hardacre's condition?"

"Condition?"

"Yes. According to Dr. Cotton, Hardacre had a weak heart and only had a short time to live."

Presently, and before the captain could reply, Marshal Thurmond entered the saloon. He carried a sheaf of papers in his right hand and a resolute look on his face. He spoke a few words with Horace and handed him the bundle of papers before addressing Andrew DuBois. "May I see your pistol, sir?"

"Certainly. May I ask why?"

"Let's just say as a precaution."

The businessman shrugged indifferently and handed the lawman a short-barreled revolver. Marshal Thurmond examined it briefly, emptied the chambers, then returned it to its owner.

I watched with interest, along with the others, as Horace perused the packet of letters. At length, he turned toward Andrew DuBois. "These are the papers that were stolen from my room. Perhaps you can explain why Marshal Thurmond found them in your room."

For the first time, DuBois appeared other than indif-

ferent. After a moment of reflection, he recovered sufficiently and said, "Really, Mr. Greenstreet, this is quite absurd. First, I was not on board when you say these papers were stolen. Second, a man of my means does not get involved in murder. It is obvious to me that these letters were planted in my room to divert attention from the real murderer."

"It is true," Horace said, "that you couldn't have committed the murders yourself, or even the robbery—but that is not to say you weren't behind them."

Horace stood and retrieved the green ball from the table, tossing it idly in one hand like a pitcher at a baseball match. "Mr. Hardacre suggested that you were a colonel for the Confederacy during the war," he said. "I only mention it because of the queer circumstance of the Union soldier's cap that was found on his head."

DuBois cleared his throat, straightening upright in his chair. "I was a field colonel for the great Army of Tennessee under General Johnston."

I could feel the weight of Horace's suspicion shift slightly in the direction of DuBois. "How did you get from St. Louis to Cairo?" he asked.

"We traveled on the freighter *Northern Star.*"

"The *Northern Star.* Isn't that one of your own riverboats?"

DuBois smiled an ironic smile, as if to say, "You are very clever, Mr. Greenstreet."

"And are we to infer that it is just a coincidence that Captain McQuaid was hired on as the new captain of that riverboat?"

"Infer what you wish. The truth of the matter is that I was impressed with the captain. When I discovered he was about to lose his position, I inquired if he would be interested in working for me. When we shook hands in the saloon, I handed him my card and told him a commission was his if he wanted it and to apply at the union office in Cairo. What you may not infer, however, is that I even set eyes on the man before our meeting yesterday."

Every murder is like a good Indian blanket, as Horace was wont to say. The patterns are quite clear from a distance, but often it is only when one looks closely at the material that the delicate and intricate details of cross-weaving become visible.

Horace lit his third cigarette, this one drooping downward at the burning end, like a wilted flower.

He was making headway in the investigation, but I, like no other, could read the worry in his face.

As he silently paced to and fro, tension and emotion seemed to emanate from the six suspects like hot cross-currents on a Southern summer night.

XXI

TURN OF THE
LADYBUG

———◆◆◆———

It was then that the tiniest of incidents caught my attention. The evening had grown warm and still, and the room close with the smell of whiskey and beer. Miss Atchison pulled a monogrammed handkerchief from her sleeve. I fixed my gaze on it for a moment, then leveled my eyes on Colonel DuBois and one by one on the other suspects gathered in the room, resting them at last on Allan Culbertson.

If the DuBois couple were involved in these murders, they certainly didn't act the part. Both had been remarkably calm during this whole affair, seemingly biding their time, as if they were waiting to see how things might play out to their own advantage. The *Mississippi Girl* would undoubtedly be sold, and it was DuBois's way to look for profit. A gold link and fetter watch chain hung from his pocket, reminding me of how impatient and eager he had been to own the riverboat. Now his face held the confident air of a man not easily frightened by the sight of a badge.

Next I regarded Dr. Cotton. The physician's unfocused eyes stared off into empty space, distant and just a little resigned, like those of a reservation Indian. I conjured up an image of the late Nellie Dawes and the old doctor together . . . I mean *really* together. He had stolen the records of his debts to Hardacre, yet I couldn't imagine him being a party to murder—especially the poisoning of Mrs. Dawes. The doctor shook himself from thought just then and, finding I was staring, rallied a weary smile.

Mary Atchison wore a long gathered dress trimmed with ruching about the neck and waist. The dress was common muslin, but the low-cut gathered neckline made it seem anything but common. On her feet were the same button shoes I had seen before in her room. Her face was not as easy and relaxed as before, as she gazed straight ahead at no one in particular.

Captain McQuaid appeared old and tired, as if time and worry had ploughed deep furrows into his face. His lips were tight, and his large right hand opened and closed at his side. A troubled look, it seemed to me—or maybe it was just irritation, I couldn't be sure. And who could blame him for either? If guilty, then he was troubled. If not, surely this experience would have been more maddening. It was ironic that even from the grave Hardacre continued his influence on the captain. He had likely missed his berth on the *Northern Star,* and now was the most likely suspect in a murder.

Lastly, I studied Allan Culbertson. He pulled at his perfectly trained beard, while his eyes darted around the room as if he too were assessing those present. But, oddly enough, his eyes again avoided Miss Atchison. I had imagined they would make a handsome couple. His right leg was crossed over his left knee, and I could see faint traces of white powdery material on the heel.

I watched a ladybug slowly cross the wood floor. It stopped abruptly when it reached Captain McQuaid's right boot, remaining motionless for the longest time as if confused. Then, just as suddenly, it took up again in a new direction.

I rubbed my cat's-eye pendant, and because I remembered wearing it on a visit I'd otherwise forgotten, a sudden flash of memory galvanized my mind. There it was: a piece of advice I'd given a year earlier, to a woman who wished to be sociable, but always got tipsy at her friends' parties. Take a meal beforehand, I counseled her, or take something to prevent the liquor from taking its effect. She was a lovely woman; that day she'd complimented me on my cat's-eye.

It is funny how the mind works. Thoughts began raining down in my mind as soon as that memory triggered them. When the final drop had fallen, I felt I had an answer not only to the mystery, but also to another question which had puzzled me as a child, one I hadn't thought of in years. The word "epiphany" appeared in my mind; it's a word whose very sound I like. I believe it comes from the Bible. But I like to think of it now as the moment when the glue seals its bond between pieces of a problem, and the whole takes shape before your eyes.

And the word "epiphany" brought back the image of my father's father. My grandfather was a carpenter. No, more than carpenter—a craftsman. With a formal education he would probably have been an architect, or a scientist. I remembered the days when he would return from work and casually mention at the dinner table that he had had an epiphany. I was small, and grandfather was eccentric to say the least, so I rarely asked what he meant. But I loved listening to the sound of his voice; his explanations were always long, and filled with peculiar carpenters' jargon—plumb-bobs, angles, and such. Then he'd say, "I just looked up and saw how the crook of an old elm fit together with the trunk, and it just came to me, Sadie." He would wink just then, and laugh. "It was an epiphany."

Now here I was, thirty years later, and having two such revelations at once. The effect was exhilarating. I had solved the mystery—and, in the very same moment, I finally understood what grandfather was talking about.

After I recalled the advice I gave to the tipsy party-goer, the memory of Hardacre's voice from somewhere in my mind echoed his words. *"In vino veritas"*—in wine there is truth. The other clues in the dead man's room were placed to confuse and confound, to obscure that one true clue. Hardacre could just as well have written it with his pen, but it was with wine that he wrote the letter "A." And I couldn't help but think he was directing that information to me, for he knew I understood the meaning of the phrase.

A series of new images raced through my mind in quick succession: the Union soldier's cap; Hardacre's unusual will; a grey shoulder cape; the poetry of Whitman.

I knew who had murdered Hardacre. And I was beginning to form a theory about the motive as well.

I looked to Horace just then, and communicated with

my eyes that I wanted to ask a question. Horace reached for his tobacco. I said, "Mr. Culbertson, you say you have been with Hardacre for three months, is that not correct?"

"Give or take a week or two."

"Did Hardacre keep another ledger—perhaps his father's ledger, from the time of the war?"

"Not to my knowledge. Except for his father's portrait, he wasn't a sentimental man, and I doubt he would keep old papers if they were no longer of use to him."

"Prior to working for Hardacre, you worked at the Planter's Bank. Can you tell me in what capacity?"

"I don't see what that has to do with all this. You will recall, I was right here in the saloon when Hardacre was killed."

Marshal Thurmond leaned back in his chair. "You just answer the lady, Culbertson. I suspect there's a good reason for her question." He said these last words as if to suggest that there had better be a good reason for my questions. I smiled and proceeded.

"Well, Mr. Culbertson?"

"I was assessor of land valuations."

"That sounds like an important title, one that would command a much higher salary than you would earn as a purser and clerk on a riverboat."

"It wasn't a matter of money; I just don't like being confined behind a desk."

Horace must have taken an interest in my questioning. His notebook was out and he was busy scribbling as he listened. As for me, I was beginning to enjoy the spotlight. I knew where I was going, but before I made an accusation, I had to make certain all the pieces fit perfectly in my mind.

"I think we should consider the threatening notes to Hardacre," I said. "The first was delivered in St. Louis. The second was delivered by courier in Cincinnati. This second note was deeply folded, as if carried in a book. This might indicate the letter was typed elsewhere and taken to Cincinnati to be delivered. If this is the case, it is quite possible, even likely, that the origin of that note was also St. Louis.

"Now," I said, turning my attention toward Andrew DuBois, "I understand that your offices are in St. Louis."

"You understand correctly," he said flatly.

"And Miss Atchison has told us she is from a town that lies just outside the city. So the letters could have originated with any and all of you, if only you had someone to carry the second to Cincinnati and there have it delivered."

I had been pacing back and forth as I asked these questions, and was glad to find my ladybug was unharmed beneath my feet as she slowly traversed the floor. With fifteen eyes watching, I stooped and let it crawl onto my index finger. After depositing the bug at the open porthole window, I returned to the center of the room. Like the ladybug, I had felt no great urgency to get where I was going. But, as each question was answered, I felt more excited and more certain I had the solution.

"Dr. Cotton. Did Mrs. Dawes speak of her time with the elder Hardacre, when she was with him in St. Louis?"

"She may have spoken of it now and again, though I can't recall anything she said that would relate to what has happened."

"But she must have known many of the secrets of the house. It only stands to reason that someone who works so long in a household will know all the wherefores and whys of the family."

"I guess that's so," he said.

"It is also entirely possible that what she knew led to her death," I said to no one in particular. Turning my attention to Mrs. DuBois, I asked, "Are you familiar with the poetry of Whitman?"

She gave me a surprised look. "I know of him, but I can't say I've ever read anything by him."

"What is your Christian name, Mrs. DuBois?" I asked.

"As I am not a Christian, I don't have a Christian name. But if you must know my first name, it is Emily."

I nodded. "And Dr. Cotton. Do you remember what Miss Atchison was wearing when she visited you in your room last night?"

Before he could answer, Marshal Thurmond stood and took a step forward. "Where are you going with this theater, Mrs. Greenstreet? You seem to be hopping about from one thing to another, and for the life of me I can't fathom the direction you're heading."

"Please, if you will indulge me just a few questions more, then I will be absolutely certain which direction I am heading."

The marshal sent an uncertain look Horace's way, but Horace's gaze was undisturbed and the lawman returned to his seat. I smoothed a wrinkle on my left sleeve and waited for the physician's answer.

"Well, let me see. Oh yes, I do remember. She had on a light grey dress with a darker grey shoulder cape. Isn't that right, Miss Atchison?"

"I guess so," she answered with an exasperated shake of the head. I could see that Thurmond was not the only one impatient with my inquiries.

XXII

THE BROMIDE
SOLUTION

———◆◆◆———

N ow, I will tell you how I see the murder of Hardacre and the subsequent poisoning of Mrs. Dawes." I hesitated after making such a bold statement. Was I so certain my conclusions were correct? Was I about to make a fool of myself? I felt a sudden panic. It was a panic I'd felt before, and my mind wandered to childhood. I was only ten when we moved to Chicago. Mother had just died, and I remember standing in front of my new class in a little two-room school on the South Side. It was my first day in the school and I knew no one. I had never felt so alone. Then, as now, I searched about the room for a sympathetic face. Back then, it was a toothless smile and a wink from a boy in the back row that helped me through. Thirty-odd years had passed. Today, that same canny smile was on Horace's face. No, it couldn't be any other way, I thought. There were too many coincidences. My panic subsided; I touched my pendant for good luck and resumed. "It is noteworthy that four people in this room stood to gain from the death of Hardacre. Mr. and Mrs. DuBois wished to buy the riverboat and Hardacre was an unwilling seller. Dr. Cotton was substantially in debt to the man. And lastly, Captain McQuaid had nothing to gain monetarily, but had just been fired by Hardacre. On the other hand, Mr. Culbertson and Miss Atchison appear to have nothing to gain. But, as Horace once told me, things are not always as they first appear.

"I believe the answer to this affair can be found in a phrase Hardacre used while giving a toast when Horace and I first arrived on the *Mississippi Girl*. *'In vino veritas'* were the words he used. It is a common quotation, which may be translated as 'in wine there is truth.' It is my belief that just before Hardacre died, he tried to communicate to us the identity of the murderer by using wine when writing the letter 'A' on his desk. This letter might refer to stateroom A, which is Captain McQuaid's, but that is likely too whimsical; Mr. Hardacre had a businessman's mind. More likely, he was beginning to write down the murderer's name when he died. There are three people here who have names beginning with the letter 'A'—Mary Atchison, Allan Culbertson and Andrew DuBois.

"As we have seen, it was Culbertson who ordered the firing of pistols and the fireworks at the very time Hardacre was shot. He also found Hardacre's body, and had a blood stain on his sleeve even though he told us he hadn't touched the body. Further, Mr. Culbertson possessed a key to the staterooms."

"This is preposterous!" Culbertson interjected. "How many times do I have to point out that I was in the saloon when the murder of Hardacre occurred? I, for one, refuse to listen further to the ravings of this woman."

Horace stared at Culbertson for what seemed like a

very long minute. He gave the clerk the look one man gives another when he encounters an unreasonable female—a look that said, "There's absolutely nothing I can do about it. Why don't we just humor her?" If I didn't know Horace so well, I would have been indignant. At length, Culbertson could only return to his chair; Horace gave me a nod as if to say, "Rave on, my dear."

"It is quite right," I said, "that Mr. Culbertson did not commit the murder of Hardacre. If I am correct about the wine stain on Hardacre's desk, it does not refer to Allan Culbertson, since it was not Hardacre's custom to address his clerk familiarly, by his first name.

"Likewise, it is improbable he was trying to name Andrew Dubois, for the same reason. But, as Horace said, there may be two people involved; and Mr. Culbertson almost certainly is one of the two—the one who had the letters delivered in St. Louis and Cincinnati, the one who stole into our room and made off with several papers, and the one who, finding Hardacre's body slumped over on his desk, placed several misleading clues in the room. And if Mr. Culbertson was not the actual murderer of the chambermaid, then at least he had knowledge of that death too. But the question remains: Who killed Hardacre, and why would Culbertson help and protect that person?"

Dr. Cotton leaned forward on his applewood cane, an unlit cigar on his lips. Marshal Thurmond coughed nervously once or twice. Mary Atchison moistened her lower lip. I said, "I believe the name Hardacre was trying to communicate was the name Atchison." They all sat or stood motionless, as if waiting for an echo. Outside, even the indistinguishable noises of men working nearby on the docks seemed to diminish into a low hum.

"Miss Atchison took a prescription which Dr. Cotton states would act in minutes and render her incapable of committing the murder of Hardacre. But things aren't always as they seem."

For the first time, a glance was passed between Culbertson and the woman in the lavender dress. The exchange was brief, yet significant. When she spoke, it was not with the same surety in her voice. She managed to raise her blue eyes, addressing first the room at large, then me in particular. "I have to agree with whomever it was that said this was nothing more than theater. Am I to understand you are accusing me of murder?"

I didn't answer her question, but instead asked Dr. Cotton, "What was in the sleeping draught you gave Miss Atchison?"

"It was morphine sulfate, one quarter grain in an elixir of bromide."

"And is there anything you can think of which could counteract its effects?"

Dr. Cotton pulled at his chin. "A stimulant would; but, you see, a stimulant would also dilate the pupils of the eye. I've been a physician for forty-seven years and I'm quite certain her eyes were normal. Such a thing I would not overlook."

"And there is no other way to prevent your potion from taking effect?"

"Not in my estimation," he said.

"Not even olive oil?"

Dr. Cotton's right hand rummaged about in his grey hair for a time; then his attention wandered to the ferrule on his cane before one of his shaggy brows shot upward. "Yes, yes," he said excitedly. "If taken first, any oil would act as a barrier, so to speak, preventing the drugs from being taken into the body." He stood, walking stick in his right hand now, his voice taking on a patrician tone. He rolled his cigar from one side of his mouth to the other. "It wouldn't altogether prevent the reactions, you understand, but it would delay and diminish them. A body would be able to carry on quite normally for some time before the effects would be noticeable."

It was Horace who spoke next. "Miss Atchison," he said, "you are—" He stopped in mid-sentence as he fingered Hardacre's will, now lying on a side table. An expression of comprehension came over his face. But he never finished that question; I had found the solution, and he was going to let me finish what I'd begun.

Miss Atchison remained still and erect as a store window mannequin. Outwardly she appeared the same, but somehow I could see a change beneath the surface, a subtle breaking down of her previous cool demeanor. "This is absurd," she said, her face just slightly flushed. "Why would I want to kill a man I'd never met?"

"You mentioned that you lived near St. Louis with your mother. I take it your father is dead?"

Mary Atchison's remote, moon-blue eyes seemed to look right through me. I had touched the mainspring of the whole affair. Allan Culbertson moved a step closer to the door, a move no one else seemed to notice. I had seen it only because I expected it. I countered by picking up my handbag. Fortunately, the little derringer hadn't worked its way to the bottom. I retrieved it and decided to give it to Marshal Thurmond instead of Horace. "Would you hold on to this for me, Mr. Thurmond?" I said. He took the pistol tentatively at first, then seemed to understand as Culbertson edged back from the door.

"Your father was a Union soldier, most likely a private, and died in the war," I continued, once again addressing the woman in the lavender dress.

Her eyes blinked several times; a sickly pallor overtook her countenance by stages. Her lower lip quavered, almost imperceptibly at first, soon spreading to the jaw and the shoulders. In the next moment, the last of her self-control was shattered as she sat unspeaking, her body shaking as if afflicted by St. Vitus's dance. A solitary tear rolled down her left cheek. Her answer, when it finally came, sounded like steam slowly escaping from a gauge-cock.

"Yessss," she said.

"For God's sake, Mary," Culbertson said, "don't say anything more! This is all speculation. She has no proof."

All eyes now addressed the purser. His features appeared contorted. He built himself up tall, then built a fire in his eyes.

It was one of those moments when one expects something dramatic to happen. Silence accumulated. For some odd reason I can't explain, I began counting slowly to myself. "One, two, three . . ." I reached six.

A grimace came across Culbertson's face; a bulldog revolver came out of his coat pocket. Someone in the room drew a sharp breath. A heartbeat passed, then two. The shot that rang out was not loud, but its effects were immediate and profound. Allan Culbertson dropped his weapon to the floor, his right shoulder gleaming red with a circle of blood.

XXIII

THE CAIRO
STATION

———◆—◆◆—◆———

E xplain? What is it that you don't understand, Mr.
Thurmond?"

"What was it that made you begin to suspect the young
lady? In my mind, she was the least likely of all to be involved in murder."

The dingy, high-ceilinged Cairo station held about a
dozen passengers, all waiting for the four-thirty train
bound for points north and east. A stern-looking President
Grant looked down on the assemblage from an oversized
portrait near the ticket window. Under it, an ornate wall
clock indicated that I had fifteen minutes to tell my story.
Like Horace when he discovered the combination to
Hardacre's safe, I felt certain that my deductions would
seem less clever when explained.

"I can't say there was any one thing which lead me to
my conclusions. It was a combination of things: Whitman's
Drum-Taps on her bedstand, the half-full bottle of olive oil,
the grey cape coat that hung in her closet. It took some time
to piece these things together. As I have said, I was certain
Mr. Hardacre was trying to relay a message when he wrote,
or at least began to write, the name of the murderer after

he was left for dead at his desk. Miss Atchison was one of those whose name began with an "A"—and the more I thought about her the more the wherefores and the whys accumulated against her."

The station master poked his head out his caged window. "The two-forty-two is on time. She'll be arriving in ten minutes." Horace left us momentarily for the ticket counter and I continued.

"It struck me as curious that Miss Atchison would be a passenger in one of the staterooms. Her clothing was of so modest a cut that I immediately thought it strange when she took that expensive compartment for the short trip to St. Louis.

"Now, if we took Miss Atchison as the who, what about the how and why? She obviously needed an accomplice, since she only boarded the riverboat here in Cairo. Remember, someone had broken into our room while we were traveling down the Ohio. That someone had a key. That someone was in St. Louis when the first letter to Hardacre was delivered, and in Cincinnati for the second. Several points made me think of Allan Culbertson. First, the way he behaved with her: He never made eye contact with the young lady, which certainly he would have if the two had only just met. Second, of course, it was he who orchestrated the fireworks to go off just after Captain Mc-Quaid made his farewell speech and everyone was occupied in the saloon. Third, and most telling, was the powder I observed on the bottoms of his boots."

Marshal Thurmond gave me an interrogative twist of the head as we were rejoined by Horace.

"It was a little trick I learned from Horace," I said, giving him a smile. "As I passed the door of compartment F yesterday, I heard voices, and I wanted to know whose they were. I placed a bit of fuller's earth outside her door—and later I saw that it had turned up on Mr. Culbertson's boots. Miss Atchison claimed to know no one aboard, so what was Culbertson doing in her room? It was clear to me that they *did* know each other—that they were probably related, or lovers, or possibly even married."

"You were right on that score," Thurmond said. "When I took her down to the station house, she admitted that they were engaged."

"That explains a lot," I said. "Well, my next task was to show that Mary Atchison could have killed Hardacre. When she first came aboard, she made a point to announce that she suffered from seasickness and would like to see the doctor. But when we visited her in her stateroom, she appeared unbothered by the rocking of the steamboat. Later, in the saloon, she seemed once again to suffer no ill effects. The fact that Dr. Cotton prescribed a sleeping potion presented a problem, especially because of his conclusion that she was in no condition to commit the murder.

"That bottle of olive oil, which she kept on her nightstand, caught my eye when we questioned her. Why would a woman keep olive oil on her nightstand? I knew that any type of oil would prevent, or at least delay, the effects of medicines or liquors. And feigning drowsiness is quite a simple thing to do. Even Dr. Cotton wouldn't be able to tell the difference. When the doctor walked her back to her room, she probably played up the fact that the sleeping draught was taking hold. Dr. Cotton left for the saloon at that point, and Mary Atchison paid her visit to Hardacre's stateroom."

Marshal Thurmond stood with hands grasping either side of his vest. "All right. Now we know the who and how. But what remains is why. Miss Atchison has been a bit tight-lipped about the particulars of the affair since she was arrested, and Culbertson isn't answering any of my questions."

"Again, it was a series of hints that pointed to her motivation. The Union cap on Hardacre's head was the most telling. I asked myself why a killer would make his, or in this case her, victim wear a soldier's cap before shooting him. Miss Atchison's cape coat was also suggestive. When we were in her stateroom, did you notice the color of the cape coat hanging in her closet?"

"No, I can't say that I did."

"It was Confederate grey with silver buttons, not unlike those worn by Rebel soldiers. During the war, it was a common enough practice for the rich to hire substitutes to take their place on the battlefield. When I read Hardacre's will, which named the soldier's home in St. Louis as the chief beneficiary, I had to ask myself why. It seemed to me the answer was guilt—guilt that he was off in England while someone was fighting for him on the lines. Hardacre himself told us he was in England during the war, and the chambermaid mentioned that the elder Hardacre had hired a substitute to take his place. That knowledge proved deadly for her. She must have told the young lady that she knew her identity and also knew she had killed Hardacre—killed him in revenge, for causing the death of her father in the war. Fearing exposure, Culbertson then made sure she would never tell anyone. I am nearly certain it was Culbertson who killed the chambermaid, for Mary Atchison seemed genuinely upset when she heard of Miss Dawes's death. He undoubtedly laced his own tea to throw off suspicion.

"The clues in Hardacre's room presented a problem," I continued, "but one easily explained. When Culbertson went up to Hardacre's room, he left a pipe nail that belonged to Captain McQuaid and a bottle of poison from Dr. Cotton's room—again, in an attempt to redirect suspicion, this time away from Miss Atchison. If he did see the letter "A" on Hardacre's desk, he probably couldn't do anything about it, since the wine had already stained the wood. He was very shrewd, diverting suspicion from himself and Miss Atchison while drawing suspicion to nearly everyone else. It was he who placed the stolen Pinkerton papers and the threatening note in the room of Andrew DuBois. He even placed poison in his own cup to throw us off."

John Quincy Thurmond shook his head. "She must have had a lot of hate bottled up in her," he said at last. "All those years to exact revenge on the man she'd never met."

"Yes, it was a long time to wait. But not so very unusual, I think. She would have been a very young girl when her father died and I suspect it was not until recently that she would have been able to do anything about it. There is an old saying: It is best to eat the dish of vengeance cold rather than hot. It was her father, not Hardacre, who took a Confederate bullet during the war and Miss Atchison did her best to reenact the circumstances. She placed a Union cap on Hardacre's head and dressed herself in rebel grey before shooting him."

"When you explain it, it does seem simple enough. But the one thing you haven't explained is that book of poetry on the young lady's bedstand. You said it was significant, but I can't for the life of me see why."

"Do you recall exactly how the second note to Mr. Hardacre was worded?"

"No, but I have it right here," Thurmond said, extracting the note from his breast pocket. He cleared his throat and read, " 'I will show that nothing can happen more beautiful than death.' Odd way of threatening someone."

"Yes, I thought it odd too. And familiar, but for the longest time, I couldn't place where I'd heard it. When I recalled the book on her nightstand, it occurred to me: It is a quote from a poem by Walt Whitman."

"Clever, damn clever." Marshal Thurmond returned Hardacre's note to his pocket and pulled out my derringer. He cleared his throat before speaking as was his custom, and tilted his head to one side, as was his other custom. "You might need this in future cases," he said, as Horace looked on with a hand on a pillar and an enigmatic expression on his face.

We all fell silent for several moments, and I realized how good I felt. No anxiety or panic, no thoughts of things lost in the past, only a sort of contentment with being just where I was at that moment. At length I said, "Now that I've told you how I came to my conclusions, perhaps you two can explain something to me."

"Anything," said the marshall.

"You had quite a laugh at my expense when I brought you on board. I still don't know what that Ellsworth business was all about."

Thurmond smiled and looked at Horace. "It wasn't exactly business," he said, hesitating.

"You go ahead and tell her, Jack. I wasn't there when it ended, remember?"

"Ellsworth is a Kansas town on the drover's trail, a wild town then—still is, I've heard. It was fully equipped for those drovers, with brothels and bars. Well, I was after bounties back then, and after a man wanted for robbery up in Iowa. I met my old friend Horace and we sat down for a hand or two of red dog with a couple of sharpers. Horace had enough sense to quit when he saw how things stood, but I didn't share his good sense. They cleaned me out. Now, I had myself set on a young lady at Lillie's Boarding House, but I was out of cash. I made a five-dollar wager with him that I could spend the night there without paying. I figured I would pay the next morning with Horace's money. Well, he skipped town, and I spent a week in the Ellsworth jail and lost my bounty to boot. That's the bare bones of the story, Mrs. Greenstreet, and that's why Horace owed me five dollars."

It was the marshal now who wore an enigmatic smile, and I soon found why. A young lady approached us quite suddenly, and I at once recognized her as the beautiful mulatto from the saloon. Again, she had on a lily-white dress that she wore like an advertisement. She kissed an astonished Horace full on the lips, proclaiming that she would never forget the night they spent together on the *Mississippi Girl.*

The train whistle blew three times, announcing its arrival. Marshal Thurmond tipped his hat to me, ushered me off to one side, and said with a wide payback grin, "I guess Horace will be occupied for a while. Be sure to give him my regards."

Marshal Thurmond stood for a time, seemingly studying my unworried face. "Well, I suspected that a woman of your intelligence would see through my little game. Seeing as I paid the young lady with your husband's five dollar gold piece, it sure would be a shame if it went to waste. Perhaps you could do me one small favor."

"Anything."

"Make him dance," he said with a wink of his good eye.

"Mr. Thurmond," I said, extending my right hand, "let me assure you your five dollars will not go to waste."

He took my hand, bowed slightly, and said, "It was a great pleasure making your acquaintance, Mrs. Greenstreet."

I stepped out onto the boardwalk as a dozen or so birds that were perched on a telegraph wire scattered in a dozen or so directions. I turned toward the Cairo wharf, where the pilothouse of the great steamboat *Mississippi Girl* towered above the other paddle wheelers; shading my eyes from the sun, I could faintly see a figure looking out from behind its high windows. "Good luck, Thomas Cooper," I said to myself, and, grasping my cat's-eye pendant, I turned to meet the oncoming train.

XXIV

LOOSE ENDS
AND REDSTOCKINGS

———•◆•———

Through a coach window, I watched the sun setting in the west. Its descent was not without fanfare; bright oranges and blues changed places with duller, yet equally fine, hues of pink and grey. We were bound for home now. Well, not exactly home; Horace had, for some odd reason, chosen to return by a circuitous route, detouring first to Cincinnati.

He had spent the better part of the late afternoon explaining away the woman in the Cairo station, while I listened with what I thought just the right touch of coyness.

He was in high spirits now, pacing to and fro in that nervous way of his which always put me to mind of a highstrung English walking horse.

He pulled a letter from his pocket. Unlike the letter that began our adventure some four days past, this telegram had no outward sign of being official business, no characteristic eye on the envelope, no special delivery stamp. Yet I somehow knew who the telegram was from.

Horace drew out his smoking gear and, in that orderly, precise way to which I have come so accustomed, began his ritual of single-handed manufacture. The end-product turned up on his lips curled at one end like a dandy's moustache. He lit it—and, strangely enough, began rolling a second cigarette, while reading the telegram to himself.

"For God's sake, Horace, do you always have to make such a production out of everything? It's from the Agency, isn't it?"

Horace raised an eyebrow mysteriously. I knew I was right. "Have you heard of the Cincinnati Redstockings?" he asked at last.

"It sounds like a dancing troupe—like the Chicago Follies?"

Horace waved his hand to indicate I was wrong. "The Redstockings are a traveling baseball club who put on exhibitions all over the country. They are, to my knowledge, the first truly professional team, and their manager is an old friend. He is rather vague about the details, but I know the man well, and he would never ask for my help unless the matter is of the utmost importance."

"Cincinnati seemed like a fine town," I said hopefully. "Are you going to take the case?"

"I'm not sure. This accompanying letter is from Mr. Pinkerton, who seems to think the case warrants two agents."

"Oh."

"Do you want to read his letter?"

I shrugged.

He ignored my shrug and handed me the letter. As I

regarded the message, I had to smile to myself. The telegraph office had typed it with a Sholes typewriter. I read it aloud:

Congratulations on case. By your telegram it is clear you did all you could to protect Hardacre but were limited by Hardacre himself. May I offer congratulations also to your wife.

I have taken your suggestion under advisement and took the liberty of contacting Sadie's editor at the *Tribune*. Mr. Chauncey informs me there are several months' worth of advice columns on hand, so she is not to worry if she chooses to accompany you again. We feel your cases have been more than noteworthy—the kind of thing Mr. Chauncey believes would be of interest to the readers of his newspaper and would also afford the Agency a bit of free publicity.

Enclosed is the standard contract of employment, if your wife is agreeable. This business with the *Tribune* is only preliminary, you understand, and Mr. Chauncey will be contacting Sadie in the next few days. Remember, anything she does write about the Agency will have to be approved by me or the superintendent. Please advise me as to your decision on both matters.

Enclosed also is a letter from a Mr. Evenson of Cincinnati who requested your services and who you apparently already know. Keep me apprised of the particulars of the case when you reach Cincinnati.

Sincerely,
A. P.

When I had finished, Horace handed me a very straight cigarette, straighter than any I had seen him make before.

"What is this?" I said.

"It is so you will not have to retrieve my half-smoked cigarettes from the ash receptacles."

I tried to look shocked, but I could feel a slight warming of my ears. It appeared that the last of my three vices was no longer a secret. "How long have you known?"

"For about six months. You will recall it was then that I began leaving half-smoked cigarettes lying carelessly about.

"Well, Sadie," he said, scratching a match and lighting my cigarette, "shall we go ahead to the smoker's coach and discuss the Agency's offer?"

"In a minute or two, Horace. You go ahead and have a brandy while you're waiting. I'll be along."

Horace looked philosophically at the embers of his cigarette. He smiled, set his derby on his head, then exited the sleeper car without further word.

He had left his Pinkerton badge on a bureau top, and I reached for it. It was heavy metal, lead or some alloy, I noticed as I rolled it around in my fingers. It had a substantial feel. I pinned it to my dress and regarded myself in the mirror. Instinctively I reached for my rice powder, but let it fall back into my reticule. The thin cobweb lines at the corners of my eyes seemed not so noticeable today. Maybe I could pass for twenty-nine. Subtle changes had overtaken me these past few days. No longer had I time for melancholy poetry and melancholy thoughts. I thought of sister Pamela as I blew out a puff of blue smoke and watched it rise to the ceiling. She'll be pleased with me when she reads my next letter, I thought. For that matter, *I* was pleased with me.

I'd miss my sister Pamela, miss my home in Chicago, miss the security of my easy chair and my books. But life is best spent on the rapids. That's what I said three days ago. I was just beginning to believe it.

I reached for my purple velveteen hat, the one I had been saving for a special occasion, smoothing the aigrette panache and giving it a coquettish tilt on my head. Removing the badge from my dress, I stared into its silvery-grey eye for a long moment. "Eye of the Agency," I said to myself, then dropped it among the chocolates in my handbag.